G

Father Bredder and his friend Lieutenant Minardi of the Los Angeles Police Department were on a fishing boat off Catalina Island when a drugged young man jumped overboard. He died in spite of Father Bredder's efforts to save him. Shortly afterwards brilliant unattractive Susan Hatfield was bludgeoned to death in the rose garden on the campus of Greenfields, a university in southern California. By an unfortunate coincidence Lieutenant Minardi's sixteen-year-old daughter Barbara, who was taking some summer courses at the university, had been Susan's roommate. The night of the murder Barbara had wandered into the rose garden, but she had seen neither the unknown assailant nor his victim. She did not tell her father or the police about her encounter there with the mysterious stranger who had talked to her so charmingly before escorting her back to her dormitory. Their meeting was something she felt belonged to her — and which in any case did not affect the murder, for Susan had been in bed when she returned to their room.

Then the first link between the two violent deaths was discovered. The drugged young man had come from the town of Greenfields. Father Bredder and Lieutenant Minardi were soon drawn into a web of danger, which threatened to entangle even Barbara, untouched though she was by whatever dark forces had caused the murder of Susan.

Here told with wit and grace, is a taut exciting story about those who had looked into the mirror of hell and the terrifying results.

Also by Leonard Holton

The Mirror of Hell

by LEONARD HOLTON, *pseud*

Leonard Wibberley

A RED BADGE NOVEL OF SUSPENSE

DODD, MEAD & COMPANY · NEW YORK

The characters and incidents in this work are all fictional and have no reference to real persons, living or dead. Any relationship which might occur is entirely coincidental and outside the author's knowledge or intent. I would like, however, to thank Detectives Tony Lukin and Larry Schmolle of the Hermosa Beach (California) Police Department, Narcotics Division, for steering me through the limbo of drug and narcotic usage. Credit for accuracy belongs to them—the errors are all my own.

L. H.

ISBN: 0–396–06486–8
Library of Congress Catalog Card Number: 79–180929
Printed in the United States of America
by The Haddon Craftsmen, Inc., Scranton, Penna.

One

"GREENFIELDS," said Lieutenant Minardi, and there rose in his mind a map of Southern California and the regions east of Los Angeles thrusting out, city after city, suburb after suburb, and township after township, to peter out finally on the fringes of the Mojave Desert. Greenfields was somewhere past Anaheim and near San Bernardino, but he could not locate it immediately. Yet there was something about Greenfields that had struck him once. He wasn't quite sure what it was.

"It's a Baptist college," said his daughter Barbara, and then with a touch of defiance, "the Catholics are just no good at cheerleading. I mean they don't teach it anywhere. I mean if you went to Marymount and asked about a seminar in cheerleading . . ." She didn't finish the sentence.

"How long will this seminar last?" asked Minardi.

"Well, it's just a week," said Barbara, "but there's a thing on stage designing or something right after, and so all in all it would be two weeks. It costs a hundred and twenty dollars —the whole thing including food and so on—and I have sixty-four dollars and sixty cents."

Minardi winced inwardly. He was from Sicily, and children who worked in Sicily came from poor families where

1

there was hardship in the home. He had been thirty years in the United States and only fifteen years in Sicily and although he had American citizenship papers and worked for the Los Angeles Police Department, Homicide Division, he was still a Sicilian. The old reactions were still there, and sometimes he thought of the savage landscapes of Sicily with its torrid summers and bone-cracking winter winds, and a voice cried out to him to go back to the place where he was born. Father Armstrong, the English priest, said that ducks had the same instinct.

"When?" asked Minardi, dragging himself out of Europe, back to his apartment in Park La Brea Towers in Los Angeles.

"Right after school," said Barbara. "School lets out on June tenth and this starts on June fourteenth. That's a Monday. But I should get there to check in at the dorm Sunday evening." She said the word "dorm" with enormous gusto. To be connected with a dorm on a college in any way at all would enormously raise her prestige among her friends. It meant really growing up and getting into the world. "We'll stay at Braddock Hall," she said, and the phrase had a great ring to her and her eyes sparkled in delight over this triumph of growing up.

Minardi had wanted to go to Catalina Island as soon as school was out. He was a widower and his daughter Barbara, a student at the Convent of the Holy Innocents, boarded there during the school year. He saw her only on occasional weekends. when school started, and he had looked forward to having her with him in Catalina, where the water was as blue as the sky and in the golden kelp forests white sea bass and yellowtail lurked. But Barbara, who had gone to

2

Catalina with him almost every year, wanted now to go to a hot little inland town instead of coming with him. Was there the beginning of a parting here?

"Okay," he said. "Provided you are sleeping in a dormitory and have proper adult supervision."

"Of course, Daddy," said Barbara. "They're real stuffy. They turn out the lights at ten o'clock and you just have to be in bed by that time. And all the outsiders will room with a 'room sister' from the college who is staying over. There's a housemother, too, and a student's council . . . and we can wear hot pants."

Minardi winced. "Everybody but you," he said. "I won't have you walking around in a pair of shorts made of a pocket handkerchief."

"But, Daddy," said Barbara. "It isn't a question of morality. It's just a style. Just because you wear hot pants doesn't mean anything. It's just the fashion."

"Barbara," said her father, "you and your whole generation suffer from one major fault—innocence. I don't think there ever was a generation on the face of the earth as innocent as yours. And that's what gets them into trouble all the time."

"Oh, Daddy," said Barbara. "It is just your work that makes you so suspicious. People are really nice—really they are."

To this, Minardi made no reply.

With his daughter due to leave him for two weeks, he wished he could find some word of wisdom and caution that would get through to her. She was high-spirited and generous and gay, and was it really old-fashioned of him to recall that there were people who interpreted these things as signs

3

of something else? Probably. But Barbara trusted everybody, and how could he warn her that there were some people who betrayed trust without a qualm of conscience? He couldn't. Whatever he said would be put aside as being old-fashioned. For all his experience in the world and his knowledge of mankind, he was in the helpless position of all parents seeing their sons or daughters off on their first big adventure. He was aware of dangers that they did not even believe existed. He could not warn against them.

He said what all the parents said, "Behave, and take care of yourself."

And Barbara promised that she would. After dinner she left to return to the convent. It was Sunday evening and she said she had to get back to study for exams which started the following Monday. But Minardi knew she wanted also to tell her friends that she was going to spend two weeks at Greenfields College learning cheerleading and stage decoration and sleeping in Braddock Hall on a real college campus.

When she had gone, he suffered through that little period of aloneness which seemed now to be more intense every time his daughter went away. He went to the bookshelf and took down a volume and stared blankly at an open page for some seconds before he realized that it was Dos Santos' *Antisocial Behavior Among the Lower Anthropoids,* a thoroughly boring book which he had read on the recommendation of the department psychiatrist, or alienist as he was called.

He tossed it aside and looked out the window of his apartment, hoping to catch a glimpse of Barbara as she got into the car. She had gone already, however, and he looked into the blaze of lights below and around him into which she had driven. That was Los Angeles. Within twenty-four hours in the limits entrusted to the police department, a hundred people or so, he presumed, would be born, and a hundred more die. One at least would be killed, two or three wounded in stabbings, a dozen mugged and a dozen more hurt in traffic accidents. A few score children would make their first experiment in drinking or smoking marijuana and a score more would try the hard stuff. To offset this there would be perhaps a score of Little League games going on somewhere and half a dozen good concerts, and in the day the beaches would be crowded and several thousand youngsters would be getting ready for summer camps.

The world, his friend Father Bredder had once remarked, is really a battlefield. The battle is between good and evil, and you have to pick which side to be on because you can't be neutral.

Good and evil—evil was called antisocial behavior these days. He turned away from the window depressed and lonely and vaguely uneasy about his daughter.

Two

BARBARA WENT off to Greenfields with a carload of other students from her boarding school who looked to Lieutenant Minardi, seeing them off, far too young to be allowed out in the traffic. He advised the girl who was driving to take the Riverside freeway, because the San Bernardino freeway was more congested and there was some construction in progress just past Covina. He gave the advice realizing that no young person would ever think of following it, and his friend Father Bredder, who was with him, shook his head in mild reproof when the car had gone.

"You're getting old before your time," he said. "A week in Catalina will do you good. They took some yellowtail off the West End yesterday," he said. "They say the albacore may come in this side of San Clemente this year."

"They say that every year," said Minardi.

"That's right," agreed the priest cheerfully. "That is called hope, and it's what keeps the world alive. The albacore are going to come in this side of San Clemente and the Dodgers are going to win the pennant."

"I can't understand what makes you so cheerful all the time," said Minardi.

"I think it's my profession," said Father Bredder. "I'm

always looking at eternity, and that cheers you up."

Minardi gave his friend a quick glance to see if he was kidding. He was a strange man—childlike, uncomplicated, and yet very deep. It was odd to think that he had once been a sergeant of Marines. "I didn't want to be a priest," Father Bredder had told Minardi. "God took a hammer and beat me into one—like a blacksmith. I wanted to be a farmer in Twin Forks, Ohio, where I was born. But I became a priest." It was a big distance from Twin Forks, Ohio, to the Bougainville jungles in World War II, and from there to a seminary in Toronto, and then chaplain of the Convent of the Holy Innocents in Los Angeles. The distance was not only geographical but spiritual, not only a measurement in miles but a measurement in some other dimension which the priest could never find words to express. Eternity did not fit. The dimension was bigger than that.

The next day the two were fishing off the west end of Catalina, having rented again the rooms they took each year in the tiny city of Avalon. They went out on one of the half-day boats and they had caught a couple of rock cod each and someone had cried "Hook up" and started reeling in a fighting, threshing yellowtail. Immediately there was a rush to the bait tank for fresh live bait and a slightly comic crowding around that part of the boat where the yellowtail had been caught, as if some law decreed that yellowtail when they appeared did so only in one spot.

Father Bredder and Minardi, having secured fresh bait also, went however up toward the bow. Here, though the height of the bow made fishing less convenient, they had more room. Lines were not so likely to get entangled and they could cross from one side of the boat to the other with greater ease should a hooked fish decide to swim underneath the vessel. There was only one other person already on the bow—a lanky youth in a khaki shirt and dark blue corduroy pants held up with a bright red scarf tied around his waist. His hair was long and tied about with a headband like an Indian in the early westerns. He was lounging against the side of the boat, his fishing rod propped up and one hand negligently placed on it. The priest decided that if the youth had a strike, the pole would be overboard before its owner could grab it.

"Nice day," said the priest. The young man made no reply other than to turn a soft smile on him. Then he reached a little uncertainly down to the deck and picked up a bottle of Orange Crush, raised it to his lips and drank deeply. He put the bottle carefully back on the deck and smiled at the priest again, a rivulet of the yellow liquid flowing from the corner of his mouth.

"Groovy day, man," he said. "Real tunnel of joy."

"In a couple of hours," said Minardi severely, "you're going to have a headache that would kill a bear."

"In a couple of hours," said the youth, "I'm going to be flying through purple clouds, man, flying through purple clouds with silver raindrops splashing all about. Purple clouds with silver rain. Beautiful."

Minardi sighed. As a policeman this was, strictly speaking, none of his business. The island of Catalina was outside the jurisdiction of the Los Angeles Police Department and, furthermore, he was off duty. As a citizen, however, he was irritated. He had come out on this lovely day to fish in the magnificent water off Catalina only to have his pleasure marred by this youngster who was under the influence either of alcohol or some drug. There wasn't very much he could do about it right away, he decided. He could report the youngster to the captain of the boat, who might be able to persuade him to lie down in a bunk so as not to endanger himself. Or he could leave him alone and just keep an eye on him. He gave his pole to Father Bredder, walked over to the youth, picked up the bottle of Orange Crush and flung it into the sea.

"Hey, brother," said the youngster, "you don't have any right to do that."

"You can report me to the police when you get ashore," said Minardi. "You ought to go below. You're as high as a kite."

"Higher, man," said the youngster. "But what is that to you? I'm in my own little old world, spinning in my own little old orbit or whatever, and doing my own little old thing. So you spin around in your little old world and I'll spin around in mine. You know where all the trouble in the world comes from, brother? It comes from collisions of the planets. One person interfering with another person. But I'm all right. I got good Karma and I love you. I'm going to look at my candle and I'm going to see that purple cloud and I'm going to fly through it with the silver rain splashing all around."

Minardi picked up his pole and said to Father Bredder, "Hard stuff. It makes them thirsty."

"Perhaps we should get him below?" said the priest. But just then there was another cry of "Hook up" and from the screaming of the line off the reel they knew that this wasn't yellowtail. "Albacore," someone shouted, and all lines were instantly in the water.

There were several hookups in a moment, for there was a

9

big school of albacore and they were ocean-hungry. Father Bredder got a bite and the line, flying over his finger off the reel as the fish dived, burned the skin. He checked the fish when it had taken a hundred feet of line and started bringing it in. It was a big one, and like all its kind turned itself sideways in the water to increase its drag. Four times it took off and four times the priest had to give it slack or lose it. His forearms and shoulders were aching when at last he got it up over the gunwale.

"Fourteen pounds easy," said Minardi with a glance over his shoulder, for he was fighting a fish of his own. "That ought to take the jackpot." Now it was the turn of the youngster. The line started to scream off the reel on his pole, and the heel of the pole jerked up in the air. The youngster had his hand on it, but only negligently, so that the pole escaped from his fingers. He was uninterested, still smiling his soft easy smile as if all that was happening afforded him only a tolerant amusement. The pole flipped against the bulwark, was held there by the reel, when a tangle of line appeared suddenly on the reel. Then the pole jerked up and fell into the water, becoming instantly entangled in Father Bredder's line. The priest's line broke and the youngster's pole was dragged away behind the escaping fish. The owner viewed it with pleasure.

"Groovy," he said. "Man, that's so groovy. Bobbing up and down out there and having a ball. That's just great." And then he was overboard himself, still smiling as if he expected to stroll over to his pole and pick it up. He sank immediately. When he did not reappear, Father Bredder went over after him. The priest was not a graceful swimmer, but he had the clumsy ability of one who had learned to swim in a water hole as a boy. He surfaced and floundered around looking for the younster, and while he was still looking, someone flung over a life ring which hit him on the head. He looked back and saw to his surprise that the boat was already quite a distance off so he was in a current which was taking him away from it.

"Behind you," bellowed Minardi. "To your right." The priest caught a glimpse of a dark blob in the water in that direction. He floundered toward it, grabbed a handful of long hair, and then got his arms under the youth's shoulders. He had never had a course in lifesaving, but he remembered somewhere seeing a curiously clumsy drawing of how to save a drowning man. You turned him on his back, grabbed him around the chest and under his arms and then you floated on your back until somebody came to help you. The full details of the drawing came immediately into his mind. Even while he did exactly what he had seen in the illustration, he recalled that he had seen the illustration on the right-hand page of some book and toward the bottom of the page. Then the boat was alongside and half a dozen arms reached out to grab the youngster and haul him aboard.

It was not easy to get him up, for he could not help himself. People shouted "Easy" and "Watch his leg" and then the youngster was aboard and a man—it turned out to be the captain—started to give him mouth-to-mouth respiration. Father Bredder had a rather harder time getting back on board, because he weighed so much. But people got him by the back of his shirt and under his arms and by the seat of his pants and he found that getting aboard took more out of him than rescuing the young man.

"How is he?" he asked when he could get his breath.

Nobody answered. The captain was still administering mouth-to-mouth respiration, but with evident disgust.

"Here," said the priest. "Let me try. I've got big lungs." He put his mouth to the lips of the young man and immediately his lips and tongue were numbed by the drug in the saliva. He blew air into the other's mouth and lungs and felt the youngster move slightly. He kept it up until his head was reeling and only gradually did he realize that it was no use. There was no heart movement and the youth was dead.

He stopped his attempt at respiration and looked up at the silent faces around him. He remembered what the young man had said to them only a little while before—"In a couple of hours I will be flying through purple clouds with silver rain splashing all around."

"Into thy hands, O Lord, I commend his spirit," he said, and the people around, sensing he was praying, bowed their heads.

Three

GREENFIELDS had been named in the latter part of the nineteenth century by its pioneers, and they had, with the gusto, hope, and bravado which marked that long-gone age, given it a name which utterly belied its nature.

For Greenfields was desert, an extension of the great Mojave Desert of Southern California. It was flat, dirt desert, formed over millions of years out of the debris of the San Bernardino Mountains, whose eroded stumps thrust upward out of their own decay to the north. The sun had beaten down on this desert for untold eons and the wind and the rain had worn down the mountains, grain by grain, to add to it. The plants that grew on it—creosote bush, sagebrush, and the strange green twigged shrub called by the Spaniards palos verde—had lived on the desert ages before the first man had set foot on the North American continent.

Then in 1867 Major Ephraim Braddock of the 102nd Ohio Infantry had come to this forsaken part of California. He claimed to be the only officer from a regiment of his state who wasn't a whisky drinker, and maybe he was right. He was one of the "Biblical Americans," that zealous, vigorous, opinionated, Bible-quoting breed that opened up so much of the American west and whose first public buildings were churches and universities. They had their counterbalance in the mining Americans whose first public buildings were saloons and dance halls. From an amalgam of the two of them came the greater part of the towns and communities of the American west; differenced to this day from those of the east which seem old, quiet and cautious by comparison.

Major Braddock, before the Civil War, had had some training in what was called in his day natural science. He knew a little of geology and a little of botany and, eyeing the growth of palos verde and creosote bushes and the mountains which rimmed every horizon, he concluded that not far below the surface of the area which was to become Greenfields there was water. He brought two men out from Los Angeles, paid them a dollar apiece a day and drilled an artesian well —having first bought a thousand acres of land at a dollar an acre from a railroad company that didn't want it.

The well came in at twenty feet, under such pressure that it threw a geyser fifty feet into the air. The water was snow-cold and as clear as glass. It had a slightly limy taste, but it was potable and excellent for irrigation.

Out of that well grew the Braddock ranch—first a cattle ranch and then, when railroad transportation improved, an orange ranch, as it is called in California. And out of the ranch as more wells were drilled grew Greenfields, named in defiance of the desert. There was a tendency in those days for men of the same religious persuasion to settle in the same area, and Major Braddock was a Baptist and Greenfields became a Baptist town. It soon had its church and its college, both of them fine structures in that Grecian temple style which Thomas Jefferson had first brought into the country.

The college, founded in open country, had extensive

grounds and a vast quadrangle, now thick with canyon oaks growing out of a lawn of Bermuda grass. In the middle of the quadrangle stood a statue of Major Braddock in a cutaway coat and slop-cuff trousers. His outstretched hands pronounced a benediction on the campus and the town, and it was a standard joke among each new batch of students to put a bottle of whisky in one hand and a glass in the other.

Braddock Hall, where Barbara Minardi was to stay during the cheerleading and stage decoration seminars, was named after the founder of the town and the college and was the oldest of the dormitories. Barbara was delighted that though the building was old to the point of being venerable, there was a modern lounge downstairs, decorated in pastel colors, and boys were allowed to use this lounge and visit with their dates.

She parted with her friends on arriving at the college with excited promises to meet at dinner in the cafeteria. They each went off to their own dormitories and she was introduced to Mrs. Mary Venables, her housemother, a loosely girdled pie of a woman with washed-out blue eyes, a lightly freckled face and salt and pepper hair which had been given a ragged cut in a desperate attempt to bridge the generation gap.

"You must call me Mary," Mrs. Venables said, smiling at Barbara. She didn't quite say "We are all girls here," but that was the depressing inference. "Your room is two hundred two. Just up the stairs to the right. You'll find Susan there, I think."

"Thank you," said Barbara. "Can I go right up?"

"Yes, Off you go. Susan will explain all the rules to you. No boys allowed upstairs—or in any of the rooms. Except, of course, the lounge."

"Thank you," said Barbara again and, taking her bag, went upstairs to Room 202. She knocked at the door and, there being no reply, tried the handle. The door opened and she entered cautiously, saying in a small voice, "Hello." But the room was empty and, alone in these strange surroundings, Barbara had for a moment a feeling of disappointment and letdown.

She put her bag on one of the two beds in the room and surveyed the place. There were two dressers with drawers and a mirror. There was a little alcove in one corner, screened by a curtain, in which frocks would be hung. There were some frocks hanging there—minis and maxis—and Barbara took down one of the minis and, holding it against her, examined the effect in the mirror. It was just the right size, a good inch shorter than her father allowed. She decided that when she met her roommate she would see whether she could trade off wearing clothes for a while. The dress was lime green and the material good and the seams well sewed. There was an expensive dressmaker's label inside.

She had just put the mini back in the alcove when her roommate came in. The contrast between the owner and the mini was remarkable. The dress was pert and joyous and the girl who came in was heavy and plodding. She wore large-lensed mod glasses, and behind the tinted lenses her eyes bulged.

"Hi," said Barbara, making the monosyllable as friendly as she could.

"That's my bed," said the other. "Put your suitcase on the other one. I like to sleep by the door."

"Sorry," said Barbara, and moved her suitcase.

"How did you get in here?"

"Mrs. Venables told me that this was my room and the door was open," said Barbara. "I knocked and there was no reply."

"You're not supposed to come into these rooms unless there is someone with you," said the other. "You're a guest here, you know."

For a few seconds Barbara fought mightily with her indignation and won. "I'm sorry," she said. "I didn't intend to offend anybody." The pudgy, solid girl appeared slightly mollified.

"I'm Susan Hatfield," she said. "I'm a senior here."

"I'm Barbara Minardi."

"Where do you go to school?"

"Holy Innocents in Los Angeles."

"Holy what?"

"Innocents."

"Oh, a parochial school," said Susan with a scornful little laugh. "Well, I hear the teaching is good, anyway."

Barbara made no reply but, having been shown where she could put her clothes, unpacked and discovered that at the bottom of her suitcase there was a beautiful rosary of amethyst beads with a silver crucifix. That, she decided, was put there by Sister Marie-Rose. She was always giving away rosaries. She spent her allowance on rosaries to give to people and she said quite calmly and flatly, leaving no room for doubt or argument, that a rosary could prevent the wearer from falling into the hands of Satan. She even said Satan, which called for a lot of smiles among the girls because everybody knew (except Sister Marie-Rose) that there really wasn't a Satan with hoofs and horns and a red-hot pitchfork. That was all part of the medieval church, and the modern church had long ago turned its back on such crudities.

Barbara hesitated over the rosary. She had about decided to leave it in the bottom of the suitcase since her roommate, if she saw it, would make some belittling comment about it. But then she decided that that was the wrong reaction, so she took the rosary out and hung it at the head of her bed.

Susan saw it and was interested. "What's that?" she asked.

"It's a rosary," said Barbara.

Susan picked it up and examined it. "I've heard of them," she said. "Magic beads. You count prayers on them. Makes a pretty necklace. Mind if I wear it? I have a date tonight."

"Yes, I do mind," said Barbara. "It's a rosary. It has been blessed." She felt that all this was received with scorn and only made her a greater fool in Susan's eyes. And yet she felt compelled to say it. She was about to put the rosary back at the head of her bed, but slipped it in her handbag instead. It was a hand-tooled leather handbag and she had spent a lot of time banging it on the floor of the convent dormitory to make it look less new.

Susan seized now on the handbag. "Gosh you're square," she said. "Magic beads and a hand-tooled leather bag. Right out of the book for young teens."

The uncalled-for jibe angered Barbara. She had an impulse to slap that pudgy face behind the big mod glasses, but controlled herself and flung out of the room. On the way downstairs to the lobby she thought the matter over. Two more weeks with that creep, she thought. And she'd paid for them—some of the payment was her own money. By the time she reached the lobby, she had made up her mind. "Mrs. Venables," she said. "I would like to get another roommate, if that is possible."

"Oh, dear," said Mrs. Venables. "Have you annoyed Susan? What did you say?"

"What did *I* say?" asked Barbara. "I didn't say anything. She's just rude and hostile and I don't have to put up with her."

"You really mustn't be so sensitive," said Mrs. Venables. "Susan's a very bright girl. Very intelligent. A straight A student. In fact she has the highest grades of any student in the college. People like us have to make allowances for people like her, you know."

This assumption of her own inferiority infuriated Barbara as did the further assumption that inferior people had to make allowances for superior people. But Mrs. Venables, seated at the reception desk in the lobby of Braddock Hall, was unaware of the effect of her words and had turned away and was looking through a card index in a hopeless fashion.

"You're a Catholic, aren't you, dear?" she asked, still looking into the card index, and before Barbara was able to reply, Mrs. Venables brightened and said, "Here we are. We had a cancellation just this morning. We can move you into Room One forty-seven in Hatton Hall—just next door. You'll like it there. The housemother is Miss Mary McCarthy. She's a nun though, of course, she doesn't wear her habit. Modern. You'll like that."

But Barbara was still boiling. She had, she felt, a legitimate complaint to make and Mrs. Venables was taking the view that Susan Hatfield could do no wrong, that Barbara was the troublemaker and the problem could be solved by moving Barbara. "Never mind," she said.

Barbara left the office and went purposefully upstairs and Mrs. Venables, her pale blue eyes mildly troubled, went to the foot of the stairs as if to follow, and hesitated there. She heard a door slam, heard a high young voice shouting, the pitch rising, and then a door was flung open and out came Susan Hatfield, her hand to her eye.

"She hit me!" she cried. "That little stuck-up bitch hit me."

A crowd of others had now gathered in the corridor and at the foot of the stairs and Susan said again, "She hit me with that stupid leather bag of hers."

Nobody said anything for a while and then a tall girl said, "What's her name?"

"Barbara Minardi," said Mrs. Venables.

"Maybe we could get her to stay," said the tall girl. "We need a few like her around here."

Four

BARBARA HAD dinner that night in the Greenfields student cafeteria. This was housed in a huge building some distance from the quadrangle—a building which had all the vastness and impersonality of an airplane hangar. An attempt had been made to make it cozy by turning the entrance into a foyer with a thick carpet on the floor and one or two armchairs about. But the noise level during mealtimes destroyed the peace needed for a lounge—the clashing of trays, the rattling of silverware, the movement of tables and chairs, and the unending hubbub of conversation.

In the melee Barbara could not find her friends. She waited in the lounge for a while, but it seemed that fried chicken was on the menu and likely to be all gone if she waited any length of time. So she joined the line and got her dinner and sat at a table close to a wall where she could keep an eye on the entrance and so find her friends when they arrived. She was joined by a tall dark girl.

"Mind if I sit with you?" she asked.

"Not at all," said Barbara.

"I'm Mary Beag," said the other. "I'm in my junior year. I should be home now, but I have to pick up a grade in American Literature and I can't make it next semester. My trouble is I don't pay attention to details—you know in putting the cap back on the toothpaste tube. And grades in college are all dependent on details. You're just here for fun, aren't you?"

"Yes," said Barbara. "For the cheerleading seminar. And then there's a stage decorating thing."

"Is that with Peyton—Theater Arts?"

"I think that's the name."

"He's really got talent," said the girl. "But you know how it is with all those people. They're all a bit weird. It's part of the scene."

There was a short silence while Barbara considered this. She understood—(it was common rumor among girls of her age)—that the theater was full of homosexuals, and she presumed that that was what Mary Beag meant when she said Mr. Peyton was "weird."

"Don't be worried about Susan Hatfield," said the girl. "She's just under a strain. She's a real brain, you know. But she works too hard."

Barbara didn't want to talk about Susan Hatfield. "What is your major?" she asked.

"Music. I'm going to teach music."

"What instrument do you play?"

"Clarinet and harp—mostly clarinet, because there isn't much for a harpist to do except with a full orchestra and then only with certain pieces." Barbara reflected that there wasn't really much sense learning harp because you never got a chance to play it anyway. Four people couldn't get together with harps and have a jam session like you could with the electric guitar. Mary Beag's next question surprised her. "Minardi," she said. "I've heard that name. Isn't your father a policeman?"

"Yes," Barbara replied. "With the Los Angeles police department."

"Was it your idea to come here?"

"Yes," said Barbara.

"Pardon me seeming nosy," said the other, "but I heard that you are a Catholic and this is a Baptist college."

"That's easy," said Barbara. "The Catholics aren't any good at cheerleading. They go in more for Latin and that kind of stuff."

"Oh," the girl said. They talked a little more about trivialities and then she said, "Well, I'll be seeing you. I have to be moving along." She smiled, put her things on her tray and moved off. Just then Barbara's friends arrived, among them Maria Pereira, to whom she was especially attached, for they both went to Holy Innocents.

She told them about her encounter with Susan Hatfield, and Maria urged her to move out of the room. Barbara said she might, but in any case she couldn't move that day. It was too late. Also she had cooled off and she felt sorry now that she had lost her temper with Susan. She intended to apologize to her when they next met.

That evening at eight there was a lecture to be given by a famous poet in the chapel, and Barbara and her friends went. They were not interested in poetry and they had not heard of the poet Kenneth Kestion before. They went because everybody else seemed to be going.

The chapel was very large, for it was a rule at Greenfields, laid down by the founder, that all the students attend chapel each morning. It was laid out rather like a theater, with a stage at one end and an auditorium whose floor sloped gently back from it, so the chapel could be used for lectures as well as for divine service. The rows of seats were of the sort common to theaters and there were no kneelers. There was a balcony at the end opposite to the stage that contained an organ and on the sides of the building were stained-glass windows.

Several people were seated on the stage forming a sort of court for the speaker, and when Barbara and her friends entered, Dr. Thomas Barak, president of the college, was making an introductory address. He said that the college welcomed the poet, Mr. Kestion, who was certainly known to them all. He was the winner of the Pulitzer prize for poetry, his work had been published in many eminent magazines and anthologies and the college was very fortunate in being able to persuade him to come and talk to them.

Then Mr. Shepherd, a member of the English Department, gave a further introductory talk and Barbara wondered whether everybody on the stage was going to have to say something. Whether they were or not, they were given no opportunity, for Mr. Kestion, a thin, white-faced, intense man in a purple sweatshirt, sandals, and black velvet pants, moved impatiently to the rostrum and took the microphone.

"Don't blame me for all that crap," he said. "And don't blame me that you've come to this white-loving Baptist-only college to be taught by a choice collection of well-shined hypocrites. You are as bad as they are because you support them with your fees, and the only intelligent thing you've done all year was to pay two dollars to come to hear me. . . ." There was a gasp of disbelief from the audience which seemed to please the speaker. On he went, piling insult on insult and profanity on profanity. He seemed incapable of uttering a sentence without malice. A tense, stunned silence in which all rustling and movement was stilled settled on the

24

audience, at first as the insults mounted one on another and all the college had stood for was ridiculed, scorned, and held up to be in actuality a means of enslaving the human mind. Then, when the first shock was over, some of the students began to cheer and applaud. The "court" in the back of the poet had smiles frozen on their faces—that being the posture they felt best became them in the cause of liberal thinking. Kestion condemned education as outdated and aimed at enslaving the human mind, denounced religion as a tool of society bent on preventing the mass of people from running their lives according to their own standards, and then lauded the use of marijuana and narcotics as keys to freedom in living.

He confessed he had been smoking marijuana for years. It had freed his mind of the chains imposed on it by an adult world in his childhood. It was his only way out of a prison of conventions constructed about him as a child by his parents and his teachers, and he had a right to use this means of escape. He then composed a poem for them on the spot to show how readily poetry came to a mind which had thrown off the rules. He composed it about one of the stained-glass windows, now utterly dark, for the exterior light was gone. It went, as Barbara remembered:

> *They made me a window*
> *of pretty colors, all shiny glass,*
> *and said the light would come through.*
> *But I looked at it*
> *with the eye of awakening*
> *And saw that their window*
> *was just part of the wall.*

The poem was loudly cheered and when the speaker had done, he was given tumultuous applause. But he turned his back on the students and, ignoring the court around him, strode off the stage. There was an immediate rush to get his autograph in which Barbara's friend Maria joined.

Barbara tried to get an autograph too because Kestion was famous, but she saw Susan Hatfield standing next to the poet in the crowd backstage and so she hung back. Susan's attitude was one of condescension for all the autograph hunters milling around, so Barbara, without waiting for her friends, left the chapel and had almost reached the vast quadrangle with its canyon oaks when she was stopped by a plump, blocky woman in a tweed skirt.

"Aren't you Barbara Minardi?" the woman asked.

"Yes."

"I'm Sister Mary McCarthy."

"Oh."

"Are you going back to your dormitory? Can we walk together?"

"I wasn't going right away," said Barbara. "It's too early."

"Mrs. Venables said you weren't happy in your room. I have a vacancy in my dormitory if you would like to move tomorrow."

"Thank you," said Barbara. "Perhaps I will move. I don't think I can get along with Susan."

"Susan is a very intelligent girl," said the nun. To this Barbara said nothing. The lecture by the poet had upset her and she wanted to be alone, so she thanked the sister again, bade her good night, and hurried off, not knowing in what direction she was going.

The evening was delightful and helped to soothe her. The

air was soft and still and cool. A mockingbird somewhere nearby was attempting a variation on three notes, and around the lamps which lit the campus roads, green moths circled bemused by the light. Barbara left the quadrangle, walked up a road with a large white building to her left, out beyond a lawn and turned to the right, taking a path that led through a clipped hedge of Eugenia. She found beyond the hedge a formal rose garden, the blossoms frosted with starlight and the air heavy with their fragrance. The rose garden was quartered by two paths which met in the center in a paved court. In the middle of this court there was a fishpond with white water lilies, pale as candles, in the middle. It was a lovely spot, and Barbara sat on the low wall around the fishpond, glad to be away from the crowds, the poet, and Susan Hatfield, and the nun in the tweed skirt—all of them upsetting for her.

A figure approached down one of the pathways—a dark figure wearing a hat with a monstrously wide brim. The figure came on slowly, one hand stretched before it, and the features obscured in the shadow of the brim.

"Peace," said the figure. "Also love and concord. You wouldn't happen to have a candy bar handy, would you? I missed dinner." The voice had a rich Southern fullness.

"I've got some Lifesavers," said Barbara. "Cherry."

"Cherry will serve," said the other. "We who are but wayfarers in time—exiles for a moment from eternity, which is our home—must take and enjoy what fruits are offered."

"Who are you?" asked Barbara, producing the Lifesavers. "You frightened me."

"A creature of the night," said the other. "In the day I'm pretty dull and am called Jerry. Who are you?"

"My name's Barbara—Barbara Minardi."

"When is your birthday?"

"April ninth."

"Aries. You are not for me. You are bad-tempered, head-strong, brilliant, independent, selfish and talented in painting, the theater, and maybe architecture. I am looking for Sagittarius—Sagittarius or Pisces. They are both home-loving, kind, agreeable, receptive, steady and courageous, and good cooks."

"What are you?" asked Barbara.

"I'm Aries like you. Brilliant, headstrong and horrible."

"Do you think I'm horrible?" asked Barbara.

"To think I must have facts," said Jerry. "Thought without fact is a monster. Legs without a head. I have no facts about you. Tell me something about yourself, and I will tell you whether you are horrible or not. But keep as closely as possible to whatever aspect of truth you are contemplating. Be rigid in this respect. What are you doing here?"

"Nothing."

"That is impossible. Alas, we can never do nothing, not even when we are asleep."

"Well, I am just sitting here and enjoying the night."

"How vastly different from nothing. Why?"

"I was in a bad temper."

"Why?"

"Because I quarreled with my roommate and because of what that stupid poet said."

"The poet—the seeker among the flowers of evil," said Jerry. "He has been deceived and he is lost. He feels his loss and that makes him a poet. At the bottom of all poetry, from Wordsworth's banality on the subject of daffodils to Dylan

Thomas's refusal to lament on the death of a child, there is loss. Without loss there is no poetry—indeed, no art."

"I never thought of it that way," said Barbara.

"Don't waste your time. I will probably hold an opposite view tomorrow. The sun is gone from the world now and so loss seems important to me. Darkness and not light hold power over the earth. But tomorrow the sun will return and I will assure you over your cornflakes that poetry and art are inspired not by loss but by reunion— the union of man and Creator. And I don't think you're horrible."

So sudden and unexpected a verdict shocked Barbara, but she managed to ask, "Why? You still have no facts about me."

"I have more than you could tell me," Jerry replied. "You listened to what I had to say and did not spurn the puny treasures of my mind. We have shared four minutes and out of that has grown a sort of immortality. We were together among starlit roses and even Caesar would have turned his head to look at us."

He bent close and kissed her lightly. "Now I will take you back to your dorm," he said; "otherwise people who have not looked upon a rose in forty years without thinking of aphids will be angry with you."

They walked back in silence. Barbara stole a glance or two at Jerry, but could see nothing of his face under the broad-brimmed black hat which was of the sort she associated with toreadors. He was a foot taller than she and as they passed the statue of Colonel Braddock, he said softly, "Good night, sweet fool."

He left her at the door of her dormitory and was gone

without a word being said about meeting again. All she knew was his first name.

The light was still on in the lounge of her dormitory and Mrs. Venables was in one of the easy chairs reading a magazine. "You're late," she said. "The lights are off already in your room."

"Is the door open?" asked Barbara.

"Yes. Nobody locks their doors here. It is against the rules. But you'll have to undress in the dark. You should be in by ten minutes to ten at the latest."

"I'm sorry," said Barbara. "I lost track of the time."

"You should be in by ten minutes to ten," repeated Mrs. Venables, seeming to derive considerable comfort from Barbara's breach of this rule. Barbara went upstairs. The last person she wanted to think of was Mrs. Venables. She wanted to think about Jerry and go over every word they had said to each other. For the first time in her life she didn't want to tell a single person about her evening. She wanted no intruders in the little area of magic in which, for the time being, she found herself.

The corridor lights were dim and, when she opened the door of her room, threw but a pallid triangle of light within which reached only to the foot of Susan's bed near the door. A slight bulge at the foot of the bed indicated that Susan was already in bed. Barbara picked up her pajamas, which she had put under her pillow when unpacking, and went into the bathroom. The window there gave a little light from the exterior and she undressed, put on her pajamas and brushed her teeth. She tried the light switch without result and, fumbling in the dark, completed her toilet.

When she got into bed, she settled down to thinking of

Jerry and the rose garden. Jerry was the strangest person she had ever met. He was a lot older than she. But then her mother, whom she could remember vaguely, had been younger than her father. How many years younger? Eight years perhaps, or even more. So the years that separated her from Jerry were not so great a gap at all.

She had closed the door leading to the corridor before getting into bed. From that side of the room came the sound of Susan breathing—heavy and regular. The sound comforted her in the strange room and the darkness and she soon fell asleep herself.

Five

BARBARA WAS an early riser and awoke in the gray of the morning to listen for a little while to the birds preparing for the day. There was first a tentative chirp or two, almost a complaint as if, Barbara thought, that particular bird's nest had been damp and a little draughty through the night. This was answered by another chirp and then a boisterous outcry as of some bird telling the others to be quiet. Then the whole chorus started, a score of voices, it seemed, all chirping and whistling away together, some scolding and others full of excitement about another day. Birds, Barbara reflected, never woke up bored, and neither did she.

It always seemed to her that something exciting was going to happen each day—something utterly and gloriously new. Today there was Jerry, whom she would certainly meet again. Then there was the drill team due to gather on the lawn outside the gymnasium at nine-thirty. Then there was breakfast in a new place where the orange juice might be entirely different and the toast crisper and they might have some strange kind of jelly that would be fabulous.

She threw off the bedclothes and hurried into the bathroom so as not to miss one moment of this new day that was just going to start. On her way she glanced across at Susan's bed and saw that it was empty, so Susan was up already. She stepped into the tub to shower and then, taught by experience, stepped out again until she had discovered which was the hot and which was the cold tap and how to adjust them. When she had the water at the right temperature, she got back in, but the stopper was down, so the tub started to fill and in trying to raise it, she turned the wrong control and was rewarded with a high-pressure jet of icy-cold water anyway which drove her screaming out of the tub.

Eventually she got everything arranged and, having showered, brushed her teeth over the hand basin. The cap to a tube of toothpaste had fallen into the bottom of the basin and she put it back on the tube while debating the exciting problem of what to wear for breakfast. Her father was disturbed by Barbara's taste, which he felt leaned heavily to the extravagant and the dramatic. In Sicily, women dressed soberly, mostly in black. Those who did not were not respectable. Barbara loved purple, orange, green, and flaming pinks.

Barbara had a flowered maxi in a silklike material to which she was devoted and which she was strongly tempted to wear that morning for breakfast, since Jerry, if he were in the cafeteria, could hardly fail to see her in it. However, a touch of caution decided her to wear instead a medium mini skirt in light green, with a white pullover with a sort of rose design in glass beads on the front, and a pair of white patent leather boots reaching almost to her knees and also decorated with a bead design up the sides. They were laced with green laces which matched the mini.

The cafeteria did not open for fifteen minutes, so she had time to walk about the campus a little. She visited the rose garden again and decided that it would certainly be her favorite spot in Greenfields. There were masses of roses, and having done a great deal of gardening with Father Bredder, with whom she waged a yearly battle against aphids and red spiders, she was able to identify a number of them. There were flaming bushes of Jacob's Coat, and mounds of a yellow rose called Buccaneer, and a tiny pink rose which was a favorite of hers and called, if she remembered rightly, Pink Elf.

She sat by the lily pond in which fat goldfish glided among the lily pads, and enjoyed the beauty of the rose garden and the warmth of the morning sun. Nobody interrupted her. She was quite hidden from view by the roses themselves and the tall hedge of Eugenia. It was a much bigger place than she had thought the previous night and she thought she would come back later and explore it.

There was indeed a new kind of jelly for breakfast—new for Barbara, anyway. It was guava jelly and was heaven's own delight on toast. And the orange juice did have a better flavor than in Los Angeles, for it came from fresh oranges in the groves owned by the university. She met her friend Maria at breakfast and explained to her why she had left so suddenly the night before, and Maria was not in the slightest bit upset, but again pleaded with Barbara to move into the dormitory with her.

"I think we could share the same room," she said. "And I've got lots of keen things to wear." She eyed Barbara's outfit. "We're still the same size," she added thoughtfully. So after breakfast she made arrangements with Sister Mary McCarthy and Mrs. Venables to transfer.

Since her new dormitory was just next to Braddock Hall, the old one, it did not take Barbara long, aided by Maria, to move her things over. Mrs. Venables, when she left, said something irritating about it being best to find one's own kind of people, but Barbara made no comment to this.

It was now time for the cheerleading workout under a determined and athletic instructor, Miss Shirley Princey, who was very nervouslike. There was no lolling around, but real work—twenty minutes of physical jerks to start with—before an instruction in steps and cheers. The morning flew by—and concluded with everybody (there were fourteen girls in the class) attempting cartwheels under the unsympathetic eye of Miss Princey, who could do them one-handed.

"Keep your rear in," she told Barbara. "The whole skeleton has to be in line or you'll fall to one side. Think of yourself as a wheel, with your arms and legs as spokes and your torso as the hub. You," she said, turning to another of the girls, "if you don't keep your arms stiff, you'll bump your head. Mouth shut so if you do fall you won't bite your tongue. . . ." **1631410**

She was interrupted by a student who said that Barbara Minardi was wanted in Dr. Barak's office. "You're not to change; you're wanted right away," the messenger added.

Disturbed and puzzled, Barbara followed the student across the quadrangle over the road at the east, up a large flight of steps to a terrace, across the terrace and into a grim, heavy building in which was the office of Dr. Barak, president of Greenfields University.

The building was dark inside and musty. The exterior walls were of gray limestone cut in huge blocks and partially covered by ivy. It wasn't pretty ivy with delicate reddish leaves, but heavy ivy with thick leaves which looked depressing. The walls within were plastered and painted, the lower half a dark green, so as not to show dirt, and the upper half and ceiling a cream color which seemed to absorb rather than reflect light. There was solemn academic silence in the building, a sense of disapproval as if the slightest relaxation of this mood might bring about the total degeneration of the whole student body. A corridor led to the center of the building, where it intersected another which extended the length of the building. The various offices of the ground floor gave off these two corridors, but right by the entrance there was a glass-fronted office containing a switchboard and a couple of desks.

The messenger left Barbara here and, glancing inside, she saw a policeman sitting at one of the desks scribbling something on a pad of yellow paper. He looked up at Barbara and then one of the women in the office asked what she wanted.

"I'm to see Dr. Barak," said Barbara, and gave her name. At the mention of her name the policeman stopped writing and got up slowly.

"I'll take her," he said. The woman at the switchboard inserted one of her jacks in the board before her, pressed a key and spoke into the mouthpiece of her headset. Then she said, removing the jack, "Dr. Barak says he wants to see her alone."

"What's all this about?" asked Barbara.

"Nothing at all, dear," said the woman. "Nothing at all." She gave Barbara a smile which did nothing to reassure her. "Dr. Barak just wants to ask you one or two questions, that's all."

"Is it about Susan Hatfield?" asked Barbara, recalling her fight with her former roommate. The policeman and the woman at the switchboard exchanged glances.

"Just go on up," said the woman at the switchboard. "Dr. Barak is waiting. It is Room Two hundred two. Take the elevator on the left in the central corridor. The room is just above this one."

"I'll go with her," said the policeman.

"Dr. Barak wants to see her alone," replied the woman.

"I still think I ought to be there."

"When Dr. Barak is ready to see you, he will send for you," said the woman.

Thus thwarted, the policeman hesitated, debating whether to exert the authority of his uniform or concentrate on his public image. A few months before he would have ignored the telephone operator and gone up to the president's office with Barbara. But there had recently been student riots elsewhere and policemen had been called pigs and insulted without the public protecting them. Word had gone around that police were to avoid any action which would hurt their public image. So public image won out and the policeman shrugged and sat down and started writing on his pad again.

Barbara meanwhile left, her mind in a turmoil. She hadn't thought for a moment that her fight with Susan Hatfield would have such terrible effects. She hadn't hit her very hard with her bag. But plainly Susan had made a complaint against her, perhaps charged her with assault and battery (the phrase "assault with a deadly weapon with intent to do grievous bodily harm" loomed in her mind), and her heart was pounding, her knees uncertain, and her hand trembling when, having knocked at Room 202, she entered Dr. Barak's office.

Dr. Barak was a very tall man in his early sixties. He had a flat-top haircut and the squareness this lent to the top of his head gave him, in Barbara's eyes, the appearance of Frankenstein as played by Boris Karloff. His eyes were deep-set like Frankenstein's, too, and when he got up from his desk as Barbara entered, it seemed that he would never stop rising.

"Barbara," he said, holding out a massive hand, "I am Dr. Barak. I want to ask you a few questions. Sit down. Why are you trembling?"

"I'm frightened," said Barbara.

"Why are you frightened?" he asked, peering at her.

"I didn't mean to hit her hard," said Barbara. "I just got mad and went back upstairs and hit her—with my bag."

"Your bag?" said Dr. Barak.

"Yes. It's a hand-tooled bag and I paid for it myself and she sneered at it." Now that she had spoken up, most of her fright had left her.

"I presume we are talking about Susan Hatfield," said Dr. Barak, who had returned to his desk thoughtfully.

"Yes," said Barbara. "I was going to apologize. I didn't think she would call in the police. I suppose she has a right to, but it wasn't that serious."

"When did you last see Susan?"

"When I got to bed last night. She was in bed already—asleep. Otherwise I would have said something to her then. The lights were out. I was late," she added, thinking she might as well make a clean breast of all her faults at once.

"You didn't see her after going to bed?"

"No. When I woke up, she was already gone."

"I see," said Dr. Barak. "You didn't hear her get up during the night?"

"No. I slept until just before six o'clock. I was tired."

Dr. Barak sighed. There had been a time when he also could fall asleep when he got into bed and then wake up at dawn. He had been a different person then, of course. It was true, now that he came to reflect on it, that he had been several people during his life. All these people had died, giving place to another. There wasn't any real connection between the gangly boy of sixteen who could fall asleep as soon as he got into bed and the president of a university who could not sleep at times until three or four in the morning. The two were utter strangers to each other.

Barbara interrupted his meditations. "Can you tell me what this is all about?" she asked.

"I will in a moment," said Dr. Barak. "You are quite sure that you did not hear Susan get up during the night?"

"Quite sure."

"Yet she must have gotten up, because when you woke this morning she was gone."

"Yes," said Barbara. "But I didn't hear her. I sleep deeply," she added. "That last earthquake, I slept all through it."

Dr. Barak smiled. "And Mrs. Venables saw you come in last night?"

"Yes. She told me I was late."

"And who saw you go out this morning?"

"Nobody that I know of," said Barbara. "I just got dressed and went out. It was too early for breakfast."

"So where did you go?"

"I went to the rose garden that is somewhere around."

"Why?"

"Well, it's a nice place," said Barbara. "And I was waiting for the cafeteria to open. What is all this about?"

Dr. Barak hesitated before replying. "Susan Hatfield has been murdered," he said. "Her body was found by the gardener in the rose garden just a little while ago. You will have to make a statement to the police."

Six

IN ALL ITS history this was the first violent death at Greenfields, and it seemed to Dr. Barak, who had spent thirty-five
years of his life heading the university, that an era of innocence had ended for the institution. There had been a time,
a wonderful time, when he and the faculty of Greenfields
could control the development of the university and mold its
character and that of the students. That time, he sensed, now
had gone. The outer world had thrust itself in on Greenfields.
Its first fruit was murder and there was no way back now to
the old days of innocence.

"What has been destroyed here in a very real sense," he
told the student body, assembled in the chapel to hear officially of the murder of Susan Hatfield, "is an essential part
of the university itself. The life of this brilliant student has
been taken in the very place where she had a right to feel safe
and protected. We will mourn her and we will continue to
grieve for her for many years. But while we mourn Susan
Hatfield, we must also mourn for this college, into which the
spirit of evil has now entered.

"How did this happen? Who is responsible? The safety of
the members of any society depends on the morality of that
society. Has something happened to our morality which has

made this an unsafe place for our students? These are questions which we must all ask ourselves now and in the years which lie ahead, for this death is the responsibility of everyone connected with Greenfields."

Barbara was disturbed by the words and turned to see what effect they had had on her father, Lieutenant Minardi, summoned from Catalina, who was seated beside her. She could tell nothing from his face. He was staring stonily at Dr. Barak, his hands folded in his lap.

Barbara had, before her father arrived, made a statement to the police at Greenfields. Her father approved of her having made the statement and said she was to hold nothing back. She had however held something back. She had not told the Greenfields police nor her father about her meeting with Jerry in the rose garden the night before. That was something which she felt belonged to her—and in any case it did not affect the murder, for Susan had been in bed when she had returned.

Lieutenant Minardi, when Dr. Barak had finished his address to the student body, wanted Barbara to return with him to Los Angeles. But Barbara said she wanted to remain at Greenfields to finish the cheerleading course.

"It's paid for," she said. "And I'll probably never get a chance to take it again. And when I get to college, I want to try out for something like that."

Minardi, who thought that Greenfields would now be the last place she would want to be, was surprised. He offered to refund Barbara part of the fee, but Barbara said it wasn't the money that mattered but the opportunity which she didn't want to pass up. She wasn't being quite truthful, for in addition to this, she wanted to see Jerry again.

"All right," said Minardi at length. "But if you find you want to come home, just give me a call. I'll be right out for you." He said good-by and, returning to his car, took a packet of cigarettes out of his pocket, frowned at the fact that they were filter-tips, broke the filter off one and lit it. America, he decided, was run very largely by hysteria. Two years ago, the whole country was being assured that smoking led to death. Now the whole world was doomed by automobile exhausts and detergents—also overpopulation, plastic containers and the oil industry.

"Chicken Little," he said, inhaling deeply. "Chicken Little has taken over the nation and is running around assuring everybody that the sky is going to fall."

He didn't drive immediately to the San Bernardino Freeway to get back to Los Angeles, but instead wheeled the car downtown and stopped at police headquarters. He went inside, identified himself, and asked for Chief Littleton. The chief's office was infinitely more luxurious than the half-glassed cage that Minardi shared with several fellow officers in Homicide in Los Angeles, but then he was only a detective. There was a picture of the President on the wall and an American and state flag on stands in the two corners of the room behind Chief Littleton's desk. These Minardi noted were new and had probably been brought in for the television interview scheduled by the chief later that afternoon. Chief Littleton, fortyish, big and pouchy, rose to greet him and held out a large but flabby hand.

"Glad to meet you, Lieutenant," he said. "Terrible business that at Greenfields. Never had anything like that before. Hardly recognize her. Beaten to a pulp. One of those maniac killings that seem to be happening all over the place."

43

Minardi said nothing, eyeing the chief's fresh linen and neatly pressed uniform. Monday, he reflected, and wondered whether the uniform would be as neat on Thursday.

"Anything I can do for you, Lieutenant?" asked the chief at length.

"Well, I came to see you about my daughter Barbara," said Minardi. "She is staying on at Greenfields and I have asked her to cooperate with you in every way and I am sure that she will. On the other hand I am anxious that her rights should be protected, and that she is not embarrassed by having an officer call for her at the campus if that is not strictly necessary. She is only sixteen and, without interfering with police procedure, I don't want her exposed to publicity of any kind."

"Lieutenant," said Littleton, "there's no need to worry, I assure you. We're just a litttle community here and we like to think of the police department as just part of the neighborhood. We think our job is just to protect our neighbors and not to embarrass or harass them—or their guests." The voice was warm, deep, and a little fruity. Minardi, conscious of the newly introduced flags, reflected that Littleton was the public-relations-conscious cop. He didn't like the type himself, but he recognized the need for good public relations, because all policing depended in the final analysis on public support. In his view, however, the best public-relations worker was the cop on the beat, and he felt that enmity between police and public had started when the police took to riding about in patrol cars.

"I suppose you will have called in the Sheriff's Department," said Minardi.

"Right," said Littleton. "We have secured the scene of the

crime and are now cooperating with the sheriff in its investigation." He sounded as if he were reading off a formula. "They have the labs and other facilities that we haven't got," he added.

"Who has been assigned to the case by the county?"

"Lieutenant Johnson at San Bernardino. A very good man." The last was said with rather a little more enthusiasm than seemed necessary.

"I think I'd like to see him," said Minardi.

"Just a minute," said Littleton. He picked up the telephone and said, "Get me the sheriff, San Bernardino," and then, after a short interval, "Littleton here. Is Lieutenant Johnson about?" He handed the phone to Minardi with a nod. Minardi introduced himself and said he would like to meet him. Johnson said he was coming over to Greenfields and would see him there.

"Supposing I meet you at the scene," said Minardi. "You have no objection to my looking it over?"

"None," said Johnson. "The place is cordoned off. Why don't you wait until I get there and then we can talk."

So Minardi reversed his tracks, driving back from downtown Greenfields to the university campus and left his car in a parking lot close to the rose garden. He did not enter the place, merely identifying himself to the policeman on guard. He walked around the outside of the rose garden, impressed by its extent, and noted the four entrances through the thick hedge of Eugenia, which here and there showed cuplets of hairy blossoms.

The hedge was expertly clipped, somewhat broader at the bottom than at the top so that the sun could get to the lower branches and promote good growth at the foot. It was too thick to get through without leaving a passage of smashed branches, so Susan Hatfield and her killer had used one of the four entrances which met at the fishpond in the middle.

The garden, besides being vast, was remote from any building. It was flanked on each side by tennis courts and at the end furthest from the road was a baseball diamond. The road which ran along its fourth side had opposite a vast lawn beyond which was the Theater Arts Building, a new structure of white concrete and blue glass with the appearance on the outside of a building from a century yet to come. It was the only truly modern building Minardi had seen on the campus. The rose garden, then, was as good a place to beat someone to death as could be found on the campus.

Minardi's inspection was interrupted by the arrival of Lieutenant Johnson. He was a Negro, which suggested to Minardi the reason for Littleton's hearty emphasis on his merits. Littleton apparently suffered from prejudice in reverse—he was warm in his praise of those toward whom he felt any reservations. Lieutenant Johnson's hair was cut so close to his skull as to leave him almost bald. He weighed, Minardi estimated, a hundred and eighty pounds and all of it was muscle. He had an open, pleasant face.

"I'll show you where the body was found," said Johnson when the introductions had been made. "Stay on the planks because we are still picking up footprints. We have seven different sets so far. Five men's and two girls'. Kind of an odd proportion."

"Men are heavier," said Minardi.

Johnson grunted. "I'd have thought of that tomorrow," he said. "How come I didn't think of it right away?"

"Too many other things on your mind," said Minardi, smiling.

They walked past the fishpond and almost the whole length of the rose garden before they came to some planks leading from the main path to the right. They were laid over a strip of lawn which formed a pleasant walkway between two beds of roses, and ended in an area of lawn where the grass was churned up by scuffling feet. A few flies buzzed over the turf.

"She was killed right here," said Johnson. "There's a lot of blood about still, as you see. She had a massive skull fracture, broken jaw, broken teeth, right arm broken, and her whole face was unrecognizable. The body, however, was found over there among the roses—you can see the broken branches on that white rosebush. It was lying face down. Those are the toe marks where she was dragged and there are good footprints to work on—the ground is soft, for these beds are watered every day, and we figure the murderer held her under the arms and dragged her in there, his feet sinking into the ground with the effort and weight."

"A man, then," said Minardi.

"Right," said Johnson. "A big guy. Like me. Those shoes were fourteens."

"I wonder why he went to the trouble of dragging her in there," said Minardi. "It couldn't have been to hide her— except for a very short time. The broken branches and trampled earth are a dead giveaway."

"I think it was a kind of reflex action," said Johnson. "If you've killed someone, you're supposed to hide the body. It's a sort of instinct. That's what he tried to do."

"No weapon, I suppose," said Minardi, getting back to the main problem.

"Uh-uh. Coroner's office says it could have been a baseball bat. That's the ball park over there and we're checking on

47

whether there are any bats missing. But that's like checking whether there is a feather missing on a chicken. Nobody knows where they all are at any one time, nor how many have been broken, and so on. When we've got all the footprints, we're going to dig everything up around here and maybe we'll find the weapon. Sure going to ruin a lot of roses," he added.

On the way back to the car, Johnson said cautiously to Minardi, "I've been looking over your daughter's statement and I'm going to have to question her again. There're one or two places where—well—things aren't clear."

"Okay," said Minardi. "I expected as much and I asked Littleton to handle it—well—without more exposure than is needed. I'll ask the same of you."

"Of course," said Johnson. There was a strained silence during which Minardi, as a father, was tempted to ask what were the unclear areas in Barbara's statement and loath, as a policeman, to pose any such question of an investigating officer.

"Anything I can help you with, let me know," he said on parting with Johnson.

"Sure will," said the other, and he gave Minardi a handshake which was just a trifle heartier than was needed.

Seven

BARBARA WAS kept rather busier with the song queen training than she had expected. She thought two or three hours a day would constitute the whole program, but the course was intensive and she and her friend Maria put in six hours a day under different instructors. She had to admit that the Protestants were much better at the whole thing than the Catholics. There were girls there from other Catholic schools and once a day a little contest was held in which routines and cheers devised by the groups were performed and judged. The Catholics never won. A group from St. Edna's did best, getting scond place in one of these contests, but then they had the aid of two outsiders from non-Catholic schools.

"It's all that kneeling down in church," grumbled Maria. "It makes you stiff. They don't kneel, you know. They sit all the time."

"No, it's not," said Barbara. "It's just that we're inhibited. I mean you have to show a lot of leg, and how do you do that and stay modest? And then you have to wiggle a lot, and you don't learn that from nuns."

"Well, we'd better start wiggling, or we're not going to win any prize," said Maria. "This is pretty leggy stuff. We could talk to Sister Mary about it."

In those three days Barbara had made subtle inquiries about Jerry whom she had met in the rose garden, but nobody seemed to know him. Of course she hadn't got much to go on—just the name Jerry and the sound of his voice with its Southern richness. She hadn't really seen his face under that big hat. She was intrigued by him and she was beginning to feel guilty about not telling the police that she had been in the rose garden the night Susan was murdered.

Of course she had been there before the murder, for Susan had been in her room when Barbara returned. Still she suspected that she really should tell the police that she had been in the rose garden and that she had seen nobody there but Jerry, and Jerry had left with her. The police, she knew, had to fill in all the blocks of time concerning a murder, and this could help to fill in one block of time concerning the rose garden—from approximately nine-thirty in the evening to just before ten. But she felt that before going to the police she should consult Jerry first, and she wondered whether he himself had already gone to the police with his story, or whether on this point he was waiting first to contact her.

There had been a great deal of talk about the murder among the students on the first day and Barbara had been the center of attention, since she had been Susan's roommate. Also there was the matter that Barbara's father was a policeman. A rumor, quite untraceable, was spread about that Susan Hatfield had been experimenting with drugs, and one line of speculation was that Barbara had been assigned to Susan's room to spy on her. This brought a rather cool reaction toward her from those students who believed in the right to use drugs. Barbara was unaware of this reaction until one of her song queen classmates, during a rest interval, asked her outright whether she was really an undercover agent for the Los Angeles Police Department.

"Of course not," said Barbara. "Whatever gave you that idea?"

"Oh, I just heard that you were," said the girl airily.

"From whom?"

"Mary Beag." And Barbara remembered the lanky girl studying harp who had breakfasted with her on her first day at college.

"Well, I'm not," said Barbara.

"No offense," said the girl. "You know how it is with the government. Why, just a little while ago they were using students to report to the FBI—getting them into different societies and paying them and then having them report to Washington. That's the kind of lousy government we've got —making paid informers out of college students."

"Well, I'm not a paid informer," said Barbara.

"No offense," repeated the girl. "It's just the way they run things."

"Who?" asked Barbara. But the girl only shrugged and said, "You know. The people that run things."

That evening there was a note for Barbara in the letter rack at Hatton Hall. She opened it and found a typewritten message on a single sheet of paper as follows:

ROSY THOUGHTS

Gather ye roses while ye may . . .
Never blows the rose so red . . .
My love is like a red, red rose . . .

A rose by any other name . . .
The red rose was beaten, the white rose had won.

J.

Only the initial on the note made any sense. It was, Barbara guessed immediately, from Jerry. But what was the hidden significance of these unfinished quotations? A reference or momento of their meeting in the rose garden? A mere whim, intended to convey an impression of wit? Or something to do with the murder of Susan Hatfield?

There had been no note in the rack before dinner, so it had been placed there while she was eating. Barbara glanced at the clock and noted that it was eight-thirty and remembered that the library would be open for another hour. Perhaps if she could find the rest of the quotations, the message would make some sense. She went to the library and spent a frustrating half hour with Palgrave's *Golden Treasury* and the *Oxford Book of Verse,* trying to complete the quotations. She found them all except the second and fifth on the list. Miss Philips, the librarian on duty, said she thought the second one was from a poem by Swinburne, but she could not place it, and the last one obviously referred to the War of the Roses in England, and advised her to try a book on English history. But by the time she got the book and located the chapter dealing with warfare between the Houses of York and Lancaster, it was time for the library to close. She left dissatisfied and, instead of going back to her dormitory, decided that she would take a little walk and think about the problem of the note.

Her walk took her in the direction of the rose garden, and

she was outside the entrance which faced on the Theater Arts Building before she realized where she was. Her first instinct was to leave, but instead of leaving she went in through the entrance in the Eugenia hedge that led to the road. She went slowly, her nerves tense and becoming more tense with each step into the garden.

The moon was almost down and the garden, with one main pathway leading to the other end past the lily pond, had many areas of darkness, with others where the moonlight smeared the grass and taller rosebushes. She walked slowly down the path, staying in the shadows, and when she had almost reached the fishpond in the open plaza, she stopped. Leading from the fishpond was a dark trail of something staining the barely illuminated flagstones. From the far end of the garden came a muffled sound as of someone scuffling among the rosebushes.

Barbara froze where she was. The muffled sound died away, but from the pond itself came a series of quick movements and a flashing of the water. Forcing herself to move, Barbara went to the pond and found a goldfish swimming on the surface on its side in the water, struggling for breath. The dark trail which led from the lily pond was water. Someone had stepped into the pond, hurt one of the goldfish in so doing, and in getting out had left a trail of water.

Who, and why? And where was the policeman whom Barbara presumed would be there on guard, since the place was still being investigated? Summoning up all her resolution, Barbara went down to the farther end of the garden. The footsteps led off to the grass at the far end, but she did not dare venture into the shadows there. On the pathway in the illuminated area, she found nothing. There was no guard and no intruder visible. Only the goldfish still flapping in its death throes in the fishpond in the center of the garden bore witness to the intruder.

Barbara hurried back to the dormitory, deep in thought. She was late getting back, but Sister Mary McCarthy said nothing about it, and she went to bed in the dark.

Eight

FATHER BREDDER back at the rectory of the Convent of the Holy Innocents was the victim of a vague anxiety. When he tried to discover the precise source of the anxiety, he was unable to do so, though it centered around Barbara Minardi. During the Second World War, before he became a priest and when he was a sergeant of Marines serving in the South Pacific, he had often had exactly the same feeling. It was a feeling of menace, of danger—not the normal dangers surrounding a United States Marine in a hard-fought battle area. To that kind of danger it was possible to become almost inured, and so go ahead with eating and sleeping and even shaving when occasion offered. This was a special kind of menace—a warning to stop and think and look about and sense, for not to do so would be fatal.

Why did he feel that way about Barbara? She had, by a horrible coincidence, briefly shared a room with a girl who had been subsequently murdered. Her connection with the girl was accidental and casual. She was utterly innocent and untouched by whatever dark background ·had led to the murder of Susan Hatfield. And yet the feeling of menace was there—heavy and not to be shaken off.

"It's probably your liver," said Father Armstrong, the

fair-haired English priest who was his assistant and held a doctorate in English Literature from Oxford. "It is a humbling thought but our spirits seem to be constantly at the mercy of our insides, and the inspiration of writers comes not from the Muse but from a well-ordered digestive system. I must add, however, that Milton was suffering from gout when he wrote *Samson Agonistes* and *Paradise Regained*. And I think Beethoven's kidneys had already started to break down when he composed his last three quartets."

"It isn't my insides," said Father Bredder patiently.

"Pretty rotten kind of a holiday," said Father Armstrong. "First of all that poor young man drowning on the fishing boat off Catalina and then this other thing at Greenfields. Why don't you finish out your vacation? Go to the desert. You're probably overtired, and you have a good two weeks coming to you."

"Maybe," said Father Bredder. "But I will have to do some thinking first."

"I'm going over to USC," said Father Armstrong. "Dr. Steig tells me he has received some early Jacobean pamphlets, printed in Leyden, probably by Henrick. He wanted me to look at them."

"Wouldn't the name of the printer be on them?" asked Father Bredder.

"Title pages are gone," said Father Armstrong, "but there were some peculiarities of the 'r's' and 'm's' in Henrick's fonts which identify his work. Mrs. Winters said she will be in about three to put dinner on."

Left alone, Father Bredder remained for a while in his study and then went to the garden which was his especial care, hoping to find some ease of mind in his roses. He had got the aphids under control by early spraying, but there were still a few on some of the buds and he took these off by hand. He had had quite a conference with Barbara in January about the rose area of the garden—whether to plant the roses in sections of red, white, yellow, and pink or whether to mix them all up together. She had wanted them all mixed up and that was the way they were, for she always won out. They looked splendid, too—a special blessing upon the earth and for Father Bredder a foretaste of paradise.

He once tried to explain that to the children at the school —explain that man alone of the creatures on earth had a sense of beauty which was a spiritual message concerning the reality of God. Animals did not have such a sense. Goats, for instance, let loose in a flower garden just ate the blooms. But man delighted in them, and in his delight got a glimpse of his true home which was in the presence of his Creator. That was what he had wanted to say. But he failed utterly and the children had laughed at the thought of goats chewing up all the roses.

He stopped in his meditations before an especially beautiful display of white roses. They were White Knights. Barbara had suggested that he plant them because she liked the name, and having been appointed head of the gardening committee by the nuns, she had collected money from the other children for the roses on the distinct understanding that White Knight was to be among them. There was the faintest tinge of green in the petals, as if the petals were really but glorified leaves.

Someone like Father Armstrong could make quite a sermon out of that. A petal might be considered a leaf transformed into a creature lovelier and greater than his earthly self. But there was no sense in his making the attempt at such a homily, for he was sure to botch it.

Beyond the White Knights the buds of a red rose were beginning to open. That was Chrysler Imperial. He had hoped they would both open at the same time.

Rose garden. Why had Susan Hatfield been killed in the rose garden? Minardi had given him all the details, and now the question thrust itself into his mind, bursting through all other considerations. A rose garden and a baseball bat. That was surely an odd mixture. A man meets a woman in a rose garden at night. Surely they met by appointment. And if so, the woman could not be expecting any harm to come to her. On the other hand the man had intended harm, for he was carrying the baseball bat. It wasn't a case of sudden murderous anger. Not at all, because people didn't walk around at dead of night carrying baseball bats. Clearly there was an appointment involved here. But wouldn't a woman seeing a man coming toward her at night and carrying a baseball bat suspect something? She certainly would—unless the man habitually carried such a thing. At nighttime?

Well, maybe not a baseball bat. Maybe something just as deadly, but less incongruous in the circumstances. But when Father Bredder tried to think of what that might be, he couldn't.

On the other hand he noted that his sense of anxiety centered around the words "rose garden." It was too lonely a place. There had been one killing there and it just might be maniacal killing. He glanced at his watch, noted it was only one-thirty, and thought about phoning Minardi. Then he decided to visit the detective instead and went out to catch the bus to Park La Brea Towers, for he had no car.

If Father Bredder had a physical guardian angel on earth, it was his housekeeper, Mrs. Winters. She was a small blocky woman of enormous determination and a fierce sense of independence. She was of the opinion that most men did not know how to take care of themselves, that priests were particularly incompetent in this department and that Father Bredder was utterly hopeless. He was a big man, needed a lot of hot, nourishing food and he didn't eat enough. He didn't sleep enough either. And she had to fight him to get his socks changed and it seemed that he had never realized, man and boy, that socks come in pairs and one sock, if not an offense to God, is an outrage to housekeepers. He would wear a black sock with a gray sock and he had once served Mass wearing a black sock and a white sock, admitting when Mrs. Winters challenged him wrathfully on the subject that although they were not a pair, nonetheless it would be a waste to throw them away because they were not mates.

"Every woman at Mass saw those socks," she stormed at him afterward. "And every one of them will blame me for not taking care of you."

"I didn't think it really mattered," said Father Bredder miserably.

"Of course it matters," said Mrs. Winters. "Things have to be in order. Surely you understand that things have to be in order?"

"Yes," said Father Bredder. But he didn't really. He understood that the stars had to hold their appointed places in the heavens, that the planets had to follow their orbits around their suns and that this was part of the magnificent perfection and order of God. But he didn't think that this extended to matched socks and seeing that shirts had all their buttons before being donned, and so on.

Father Bredder put his head through the kitchen door before departing to tell Mrs. Winters that he was going and she told him to be sure to be back for dinner at six-thirty promptly. She had a silverside of beef, cabbage and potatoes, and it wasn't the kind of dinner that could be kept waiting. There would also be rice pudding, she added with a deal of malice, it seemed to the priest, for it was a hot day and more suited to ice cream.

Mrs. Winters did the marketing for the rectory. She had to market on a very small budget because Father Bredder took his vows of poverty very seriously and tried to save on his budget and give the surplus to some good cause. It was lucky that the city market, where food was sold at wholesale, was close to the convent or Mrs. Winters just wouldn't have been able to feed the two priests on the amount available.

Father Bredder kept no more than fifteen dollars a month for himself, and he often gave a dollar or two of that away to his friends on nearby Main Street, whom Mrs. Winter, he knew, held to be winoes and drug users and no-goods. He allowed himself one or two pipes of tobacco a day, and smoked a dark, coarse Carolina tobacco which he kept in a paper envelope because he didn't think he ought to buy a tobacco pouch. During Lent he gave up smoking, took only one meal a day and that not a full one, and wherever he had to go he walked.

"He takes being a priest so seriously, you'd think it was more important than being President," Mrs. Winters stormed once to Sister Theresa, who was the Reverend Mother at the convent. And then she had been surprised by the realization that Father Bredder actually did think being a priest was more important than being President.

"Well," said Mrs. Winters, reflecting somewhat savagely on Father Bredder's shortcomings after he had gone, "his being a priest saved some poor woman from marrying him. There never was a man who could do so many things wrong about a house. Never."

These angry thoughts were quite a comfort to Mrs. Winters, whose dinner was jeopardized by the priest's decision to visit his friend Lieutenant Minardi. She had worked herself up into quite a good humor with her anger, and had put the beef on to boil, when the front door bell rang, irritating her all over again, for she disliked callers when she was cooking.

She opened the door to find a tall, lanky man dressed in a blue corduroy coat with large silver buttons and yellow canvas sailor pants standing there. "Bredder in?" he asked.

"Do you mean Father Bredder?" snapped Mrs. Winters, who didn't like hippies.

"Is he around?" asked the visitor, ignoring the correction.

"No, he's not. What do you want?"

"I want to see him."

"About what?"

"Man," said the visitor, ignoring Mrs. Winters' sex, "we could keep this going for a year. Just words. You say some words and I say some words. You're living in your little castle and I'm out here in the woods. It's a waste of time. But then what's time? I'll tell you what it is, it's a great lump of boredom that lies between nothing and nothing. It's nothing disguised as something, the void parading as substance. . . ."

"My beef is boiling right in the middle of that nothing disguised as something you're talking about," snapped Mrs. Winters, and made to close the door.

"Tell him to call me when he gets in. I'm staying at the Hilton," said the visitor. He fished a number of visiting cards out of the breast pocket of his blue corduroy jacket. They were of different colors—some orange, some purple, some pink, some black with pale blue lettering. "Tuesday," he said, and the "fifteenth hour. Pink and silver should be right." He gave a pink and silver card to Mrs. Winters.

"You are about to disappear," he said solemnly and walked away, leaving Mrs. Winters staring after him. When he had gone, she sniffed the card. Years of cooking and marketing had provided her with this simple test of whether something was wholesome or not. The card smelled of flowers—roses. She took it into the kitchen and put it up against a large coffee can containing bacon fat. It would soon smell of bacon grease, she reflected, as she turned to the beef. That would be an improvement.

Father Bredder meanwhile found Minardi in the large living room of his apartment at Park La Brea Towers. The door was opened for him by Bob Dew, Minardi's personal servant, who was also on parole from San Quentin. He was a tough, outspoken man, with an insatiable curiosity which he did not attempt to disguise. His thin hair was sandy in shade and his round face displayed a few pale freckles, the sum total of all the pigmentation his body could conjure up. He adored Barbara Minardi and there was between the girl and the convict an immediate understanding which Minardi

62

was at a loss to explain. He had taken Bob Dew on as a personal servant to train him in household work, since outdoor work, particularly in California, where he had to stay, gravely affected his pigmentless skin, and office work was beyond him. He kept him because of his affection for Barbara, who had at times to be alone in the apartment. Bob Dew was both a bodyguard and companion for her. He was sure he would no more hurt Barbara than a Saint Bernard dog would.

"Come on in," said Bob. "He's getting ready to run for President."

"He's what?" asked Father Bredder.

"See for yourself. He's taken up golf. Used to hafta' wear an Indian bonnet. Now you play golf with film stars." Minardi was in the living room looking over a gleaming set of golf clubs.

"Just got them," he said. "You play?"

Father Bredder shook his head. "I used to caddy when I was a boy. Back in Twin Forks. Only rich people played." And then he was sorry he had said that, because it sounded as if he resented some people being rich, and he didn't at all. He knew a lot of the things he said gave wrong impressions and he wished he could develop some agility in speech, but he couldn't. He picked up a club which he remembered as a driver and looked it over. "They certainly changed these," he said. "The shaft used to be of hickory. And there was a little lead weight sometimes under the head. I didn't think they'd changed so much."

"You know what's odd," said Minardi. "They still call them clubs. There is a direct line between this and what the Neanderthal used for beating a bear's brains out. Odd, isn't it? A baseball bat, which looks like a club, is called a bat. But a golf club, which doesn't look like a club at all, is still called a club."

"Were you thinking of the girl at Greenfields?"

"Vaguely," said Minardi.

The priest nodded. "I had been wondering about someone meeting a girl in a rose garden and carrying a baseball bat —at nighttime," he said. "I suppose a golf club would be less hostile-looking? What do you think?"

Minardi shrugged. "I asked our coroner to contact the San Bernardino County cornoner and get a report. He said a heavy, rounded instrument—most of them say blunt. The head of this is heavy but not rounded. It has a face and definite corners."

Father Bredder picked up the driver. It seemed to immediately shrink in his huge hands. He swung it through the air once or twice and shook his head. "No," he said. "Something short. This wouldn't do."

"I agree," said Minardi. "The reason people don't get killed with golf clubs is not that golfers are not murderous but that you have to take too big a swing. Now a croquet mallet . . ."

"There are corners on them," said the priest.

"I just don't like the baseball bat," said Minardi.

"Nor I," said the priest. "It is the wrong thing to be carrying at night in a rose garden. Even a ball player doesn't walk around with a baseball bat. And if the killer brought a baseball bat with him, surely Susan Hatfield would have run from him."

"What was the immediate or prime cause of death?"

"Brain damage. There was one blow so tremendous that

it crushed the skull like an eggshell and destroyed a vital area of the brain. There were many more blows, some after that and some before. The pathologist says at least three before, and half a dozen afterwards."

"How would he know?" asked the priest.

"Well, when the heart stops pumping, there is no further bleeding other than a gravity flow of blood which is very small. It seems to have been a maniac attack. Even the pelvic bones were fractured up by the hip joint. And they're tough."

"Before or after she died?" asked the priest.

Minardi shrugged. "I didn't ask," he said. "Do you think it matters?"

"I don't suppose so," said the priest. "It's so savage. That's what disturbs me. It seems like a murder of madness but for one thing."

"What's the one thing?" asked Minardi.

"The rose garden," said the priest. "I feel that people don't go into places like rose gardens at nighttime unless they have an appointment there. And if a young girl has an appointment in a rose garden at nighttime, surely it would be with a boy friend whom she knew well, and not with a maniac."

"You haven't seen it, have you?" said Minardi. "Even during the day I would say it was isolated. It's immense— worth walking around. A good place for lovers' trysts—or murder."

"You should warn Barbara to stay away from it," said the priest suddenly. "If we are dealing with a maniac, it is a dangerous place, and she is very fond of roses."

"I warned her," said Minardi, and then he added, "but I'm only her father."

"You got to tell her," said Bob Dew, who had been listening unashamed to the conversation. "San Quentin is full of kids that never got told until it was too late. Next time you see her, tell her I say stay out of that rose garden—or else."

"Or else what?" asked Minardi.

"Or else I won't take her on a tour of the joints on Main Street no more," said Bob. "That's what."

Nine

FATHER BREDDER persuaded Minardi to come and have dinner with him at the rectory. Minardi suggested they dine at his apartment, but Father Bredder dared not tell Mrs. Winters he would not be home for dinner. She would be very annoyed, and rightly so. So they returned together in Minardi's car to the Convent of the Holy Innocents and Minardi, as they pulled inside the gate to the rectory with the rose garden behind it, said, "Why do I always have a kind of guilty feeling whenever I come to this place?"

"I never feel quite comfortable in a police station," confessed Father Bredder. "Perhaps it is the same kind of thing."

"You stole apples from people's orchards when you were a boy?" asked Minardi.

"Oh, yes," said Father Bredder. "The best apples I ever ate were stolen."

"Well, you pay for them every time you enter a police station," said Minardi. "At least that is what a psychologist would tell you. But why should I feel uncomfortable when I come here?"

"When you have found out, I will hear your confession, if you wish," said Father Bredder with the ghost of a smile.

Mrs. Winters was pleased that Father Bredder had brought a guest. If she had one vocation in life, it was to feed men. She liked to make great boiled dinners for them and have the dinners eaten with gusto. Father Bredder was a moderate eater. Father Armstrong ate as a matter of duty, for he never seemed to be hungry. Minardi, however, was a good eater and despite the heat of the day, he welcomed a boiled dinner since, as a bachelor, most of his dinners were roasted, grilled or fried. Minardi then ate well and Mrs. Winters was pleased with him though she could not resist asking, knowing he was a policeman, when he was going to clean up the city of all the "long-haired oddballs" and "no-goods" who had invaded the place.

"They should all be in jail," said Mrs. Winters. "The President should pass a law forbidding boys to wear long hair."

"What good would that do?" asked Father Bredder.

"People who wear tiger skins behave like tigers. And if you take the skin away from them, they have to behave just like decent folk. That's what good it would do." And to reprimand the priest for asking so silly a question, she put another spoonful of boiled carrots on his plate.

When she had gone, Father Armstrong said, "Isn't it amazing that somebody can live in this country for half a century and not know that the President doesn't make laws?"

"What is odder," said Father Bredder, "is that Presidents can live in this country and not know that they are made by people like Mrs. Winters." He wanted to talk about the murder, but instead asked Father Armstrong how he had fared at the USC library. Father Armstrong said he had had an interesting afternoon. The library had acquired, at an auction in Antwerp, a bale of printed matter which contained many examples of fifteenth- and sixteenth-century printing and filled in many gaps in its collection of examples of European printing.

"Just printing?" asked Father Bredder. "What was the subject matter?"

"Oh, the usual amusing childish nonsense," said Father Armstrong. "How to turn quicksilver into gold, how to interpret omens. There's masses of that stuff available, you know. People have always made a living out of it. In fact there is a revival of interest in it among young people now, as you know. Astrology, alchemy, charms, omens, witches, succubuses, black masses—half of the world is headed for the moon and the other half back to the Middle Ages. I'm told there is a black mass held in Los Angeles every night." He glanced at Minardi. "Would that be so?" he asked.

Minardi shrugged. "I'd be surprised if there is only one," he said. "Satanism is a growing cult. I don't know," he added, "whether this is the concern of my profession or yours."

Father Armstrong got up slowly from the table and said quite seriously, "Any day now I expect to be called in to cast out a devil. I hope that I will be adequate."

Minardi and Father Bredder retired to the priest's study after dinner to continue their talk on the Greenfield's murder. "What is known about the girl?" asked Father Bredder.

"A great deal, and yet not enough," said Minardi. "Age twenty-two, parents divorced, living officially with her mother in Pawtucket, Rhode Island. Actually the mother has remarried, and is often away from home with her present husband. She was in Italy when her daughter was killed, but got back for the funeral. She had not seen the daughter for several months. Susan Hatfield really did not have a home, though she had an address—at Pawtucket, Rhode Island. Before college she was at a boarding school. Not much home life for her, it would seem, since her mother and father were divorced. She was ten then."

"Who paid her fees?" asked Father Bredder.

"Her mother. They were paid up ahead of time."

"What about her father?"

"Kenneth Hatfield. If he is still alive, he will be sixty years of age. Married a little late and was some years older than his wife. He lives vaguely in South America—Chile, Argentina. Somewhere there. The mother doesn't know."

"Was Susan Hatfield a drug user?" asked the priest.

"No, she wasn't," said Minardi. "The coroner's office says there is no evidence of drug use, though she may have used marijuana now and again. We don't know enough about its effects to decide in the case of light users."

"Was she hard put for money?"

"No. Her tuition and board were paid by her mother. In addition she had a bank deposit of two hundred dollars a month to her credit, again made by her mother. She hadn't a car and with everything paid she would have a hard time getting rid of two hundred dollars a month. In fact her bank balance is around a thousand dollars. She had eighteen dollars in her handbag, which was in her room, and some stamps, twenty-one-cent and seventeen-cent airmail stamps."

"Boy friends?" asked the priest.

"She wasn't very attractive," said Minardi. "But she had

money. I don't think she lacked companionship. She spent most of her time studying, however. She was the top student at Greenfields and carried a big load."

"What was her major?"

"Chemistry," said Minardi. "Inorganic chemistry. About as dull, I would think, as she could find. But to relieve the tedium, I suppose, she had credits in Comparative Theology, Social Anthropology, Medieval History, and Theater Arts."

"No botany?" asked the priest.

"Uh-uh."

Father Bredder shook his big head, mystified. "What do you make of it?" he asked.

"Too soon for one to say anything," said Minardi. "I just get all the evidence together and then start sorting it out into colors and shapes. I'm not even ready to think about it right now. Let me ask a question. What do *you* think of it?"

"I think I understand her," said Father Bredder. "She comes from a broken home in which there is money available but no love for her. She goes to a college as remote as can be found from her home—a college in California and her home is in Rhode Island. She found no love at home and went as far from it as she could—to forget that there was no love there. In college she buried herself in work. Not just to fill up the emptiness but to try to find why she wasn't loved. Many people do that. They turn to science not for knowledge but to console themselves by proving that love—and God—don't exist. They have to prove that to account for their own rejection. And of course it is impossible. If Susan Hatfield had been more attractive and less intelligent, she might have tried to find love as so many rejected children do these days —making themselves freely available to anybody who wants them, even for a passing moment. Of course that isn't really love. But for a while they believe it is. And yet . . . To give yourself to someone for whom you don't really care; to do this to lessen their loneliness. I think God would understand that. . . .

"You are getting perilously close to prostitution," said Minardi.

"No," said the priest. "I'm not. The prostitute doesn't give. She takes. But these children give—or try to give. They are wrong in what they do, but in what they are trying to do they are right. The first crime in the world was the denial of love—and the world is still suffering from it."

"Getting back to Susan Hatfield," said Minardi. "You have a lonely, loveless, plain lump of a girl with a good mind, living as far away as she could from an unpleasant home, studying things to explain her state and becoming a brilliant scholar. Okay. I'll buy it. But why does someone beat her brains out with a baseball bat?"

"That's another girl," said Father Bredder. "That's another girl entirely and one we don't know anything at all about."

"We know something about her," said the detective. "We know that she got Barbara so mad she hit her with her handbag. Barbara doesn't fly off the handle like that. Susan Hatfield had an ability to provoke rage in people."

"Yes," said Father Bredder thoughtfully, "and that is a different person from the lonely girl trying to compensate for being unloved."

"There are two other items I might as well mention to you," said Minardi. "Maybe they have something to do with the case. Maybe they don't. The first is that when Barbara

72

mentioned she was going to Greenfields, I remembered having seen that name somewhere in a report, but I could not recall the connection. Now I know what it was. The report was from Sacramento and dealt with narcotics arrests in California. Greenfields was listed as one of the few towns in Southern California in which no narcotics arrests had been made for several years—I think it was five years. That's the first item. The second was a report from the sheriff's department about that man who jumped overboard and ruined our fishing trip. His name was Edward Smith. He was a short-order cook and he worked at the Green Bay Tree Café at—guess where?"

"Greenfields," said Father Bredder.

"Greenfields," said Minardi. "A nice neighborly little place, as the police chief once told me, with no record of narcotics arrests for several years."

Ten

IT WAS THE FOLLOWING DAY before Mrs. Winters remembered to tell Father Bredder about the caller with the pink and silver visiting card. She picked it up from behind the coffee can of bacon grease against which she had propped it, and plumped it down on the table while the priest was having breakfast.

"That called for you yesterday," she said. "Smells of flowers," she added, as if this constituted a grave measure of guilt. The priest examined the card. Printed on it, in Gothic characters, was the name Kenneth Kestion and nothing else. He sniffed the card. The fragrance was still triumphant though the aroma of bacon grease was beginning to intrude.

"Did he leave a message?" asked Father Bredder. Mrs. Winters never volunteered any information. Everything had to be dredged out of her by questions.

"No. Except that he wanted to see you."

"Did he leave an address?"

"He said he was staying at the Hilton."

"And that was all?"

"And enough, too," said Mrs. Winters.

"Was he young or old?" asked Father Bredder, trying to recall who Kenneth Kestion might be. The name was vaguely familiar.

"He had long hair," said Mrs. Winters. "And a silly jacket with big silver buttons. And he said I was going to disappear."

Father Bredder glanced at Father Armstrong and the latter picked up the card and exclaimed, "Kenneth Kestion. I say, you do have the most remarkable acquaintances. He won the Pulitzer prize for poetry. This is the greatest songbird of soul the country has yet produced. Are you going to see him?"

"I don't know," said Father Bredder.

"Oh, you've got to," said Father Armstrong. "Heavens, Kestion is the darling of student bodies across the continent. They love him. He lectures everywhere and for huge fees. Students get such a lift out of all the cesspool words being said right out there aloud before their impotent faculty on the campuses. He's a sort of Cloaca Maxima of the puritan mind. All that is revolting and must be got rid of flows right through him, and everybody feels liberated afterwards."

It was only then that Father Bredder recognized Kestion as the poet who had lectured at Greenfields the night that Susan Hatfield was murdered. He called him after breakfast and Kestion said that he could see Father Bredder at two that afternoon.

"I can't see you at that time," said Father Bredder. "I am hearing confessions at the cathedral from two to four. I can see you at noon or about five."

"Two is the only favorable hour in the whole day," said Kestion. "It has to be two o'clock. It can't be any other time. Can't you forget about confessions or get someone else to do the forgiving? All that guilt crap is medieval anyway."

"It's much older than that," said Father Bredder simply. "It goes right back to the time when man ceased to be a beast and recognized right and wrong."

"Christ," said Kestion, and the priest shuddered. "You're really locked in the Dark Ages."

"Why can't you see me at noon?" asked Father Bredder.

"Because my horoscope says two is the only favorable hour," replied Kestion.

"Why do you object to the Middle Ages if you're run by the Assyrians and Babylonians?" asked the priest. "I will be glad to see you at noon or at five, but I cannot see you at any other time."

"Just a minute." There was a silence and then Kestion, having apparently looked up his forecast for the day, said, "How about eleven minutes to one—here?"

"The time is all right, but you must come here."

"Oh . . . you," said Kestion and hung up.

"Did you say he was a poet?" asked Father Bredder, turning to Father Armstrong.

"Yes. He has talent and could be a great poet if pandering to the student mind wasn't such a lucrative temptation. He wrote some things many years ago which were particularly fine. I remember one especially.

"How dark lies beauty on the mind
Forever hidden in the void
And trembling there beyond my sight.
Life is not day but blackest night
And breath but death disguised.

"The internal rhyming of breath and death is Celtic and the whole concept I find profoundly moving. It reminded me of some aspects of St. John of the Cross."

"He really wrote that?" asked Father Bredder.

"Yes. But he got his fame and his awards for graffiti and pornography. I say that without linguistic bias, for pornography is, of course, an attitude of mind and not just words. . . ." But Father Bredder wasn't listening. The words

Life is not day but blackest night
And breath but death disguised

had struck him like a blow. He reached for the telephone directory, looked up the number of the Hilton, dialed and asked for Kestion.

"I want to apologize," he said. "I will meet you at your hotel if you wish at ten minutes to one."

"What brought that on?" asked Father Armstrong, mystified.

"I am a very stupid man," said Father Bredder. "And often don't realize when people are dying."

Kestion occupied a large suite on one of the upper floors of the Hilton. There was a spacious living room whose dove-gray deep-pile carpet was strewn with newspapers and magazines when the priest entered. Two color television sets were turned on to two different programs and placed before a circular overstuffed couch. Kestion had been sitting on the couch seemingly trying to watch the two programs at once, and in addition to this a record was being played on a phonograph so that as soon as Kestion opened the door, the priest found himself shrinking from the babble of sound to which the poet seemed oblivious.

"Could we have a little quiet?" he asked, and Kestion somewhat sulkily turned off the two television sets but left the record player operating.

"It's the fuzz," said the poet. "They've been asking me quesions about that stupid pig of a girl who had her brains bashed in at the squalid little college I spoke to. They think I did it."

"Did you?" asked Father Bredder.

"Christ, no," said Kestion. "I don't have to kill people with baseball bats. I'm not a Neanderthal. I'm a poet. Anyway, I couldn't stand beating somebody's brains in. Or maybe I could. Maybe killing is the supreme act of self-expression which, denied to man, has driven him mad. Maybe we would all be saner if we were allowed to kill someone once in our lives."

"Do you have an alibi?" asked Father Bredder.

"I hate the goddam word," said Kestion. "It's ugly. It has an ugly sound. And I do not. I got away from those leeches looking for autographs with that dull girl. I stopped the car in some godforsaken orange grove, but she said she didn't feel like it, so I kicked her out and drove back to town."

"Right back?"

"To Santa Monica."

"Why?"

"Listen, Bredder, since nothing in the world makes any sense, absolutely no sense at all, what is the use of asking questions? Are you in eager search of the worthless, the spurious, the asinine non sequiturs which constitute what you call life? I am only sitting here making noises at you

78

because the fuzz think I killed that pig of a girl."

"Why did you go to Santa Monica?" asked Father Bredder.

"Because my horoscope said I should. At midnight. It was propitious for me to meet a stranger. And that stranger wasn't apparently that dull girl. So I decided it was the Pacific Ocean and I went to Santa Monica and walked into the ocean to meet the stranger which was the ocean. It was as cold as hell."

"In your clothes?"

"Yes," said Kestion. "In my clothes."

"Why?"

"Because I had never walked into the ocean in my clothes before."

"So you were soaking wet when you came back to the hotel?"

"No. I always have three or four suits in the car. Anybody can tell you that a Capricorn should not wear the same color for more than three hours or vital energy will be drained from him."

"What did you do with the wet clothes?"

"I threw them away."

"Where?"

"Into the ocean—where else?"

"So you drove off with Susan Hatfield," said Father Bredder, "and she was found murdered. You were the last person who was seen with her. You have no alibi for several hours after leaving with her. And you threw away the clothes you were wearing. That looks very suspicious."

"That's what the dark stranger told me," said the poet.

"The dark stranger?"

"The black detective in the sheriff's department or whatever they call it out there. And he may hurt me. He's Pisces, and the Goat and the Fish are inimical signs."

"What do you want me to do?" asked the priest.

"Find whoever it was that killed that placid virgin. The police won't. They've found me. They only have to cook up the evidence and find a motive and they'll arrange for my death."

"Are you telling me the truth when you say you did not kill her?" asked Father Bredder gravely.

"Of course I am," said Kestion. "Although in a sense I did kill her—when I kicked her out of the car in return for her frigidity. That's a form of murder, you know. To deny a woman all prospect of intercourse with you is to murder her. But in the same sense she murdered me first. But I didn't bash her brains in with a baseball bat."

"Until the police find a motive, they haven't got a real case against you," said Father Bredder.

"Look Bredder," said Kestion. "Why do you keep insisting that things have to make sense? They don't. All the police have to find out is that I use drugs, which will be very easy, and they have a case. I killed her in a frenzy produced by smoking marijuana. Or whatever."

"Do you use narcotics?"

"Of course I do. Don't you?"

"No."

"Naturally. You live in the Dark Ages. I am a child of light." He glanced at a watch held around his neck on a gold chain and said, "I can't talk to you any more now. The bad time is coming. What is your fee?"

"I have no fee," said the priest.

80

"Oh, Christ, I can't stand your unctuous piety. Everybody has a fee or they don't work. What is yours?"

"I have none," said the priest. "I do not know even if I can help you. But your danger isn't from the police, but from elsewhere. And I will pray for you." He closed the door, leaving Kestion staring after him.

Eleven

LIEUTENANT LEROY JOHNSON of the San Bernardino Sheriff's Department was watching a fly buzzing against the window in Dr. Thomas Barak's office. The fly had no concept of glass. If it had any understanding at all, that understanding did not extend to identification of the invisible, transparent yet solid matter which intervened between itself and the outside air. It was flying as hard as it could, trying to get through the window, but only going up, down, and sideways —never forward. If the fly had any mentality, Lieutenant Johnson mused, it would, according to the psychologists, eventually become frustrated and refuse to make any effort at all. But the fly had no mentality, so it could not be frustrated and would keep on trying. Until it died? What would happen if you put a fly in a box made entirely of glass? Would it exhaust itself trying to get out? Or would it just adjust to the fact that something had gone wrong with the air and it could not fly any distance in any direction?

"She will be here in a few minutes," said Dr. Barak, replacing the telephone. "In the meantime, is there anything you want to tell me or that I can tell you in her absence?"

"I've been over everything that is available to me on Susan Hatfield," said the lieutenant. "And I can't find any reason at all why she should have been beaten to death. Can you make any suggestions?"

The question, put so suddenly, left Dr. Barak without words for a moment. "She was a model student," he said. "An excellent worker. I can think of no reason at all."

"That's another pane of glass," said the lieutenant. "Was she ever in any trouble—did she ever have to be disciplined?"

"Nothing of that nature has ever come to my attention."

"Would it come to your attention?"

"Not unless it was a serious matter."

"Would the use of narcotics be a serious matter?"

Dr. Barak was immediately offended. "We have never had even a suggestion of the use of narcotics on this campus," he said.

"Dr. Barak," said Lieutenant Johnson. "There is not a college campus in the United States of America nor a high school where someone is not experimenting with narcotics. Greenfields is no exception. The people who do the experimenting are usually the bright students. Not always, but usually. Or people who want to be thought of as bright. It's a sign of intelligence to kick your mind about."

"Nonetheless," said Dr. Barak firmly, "nothing of that sort has ever come to my attention—and I assure you it would come to my attention—on this campus."

"Then you all better have a meeting with your faculty and question them, because somebody is covering up," said the lieutenant. "Like I said, there isn't a campus in the country that is that clean."

Dr. Barak said nothing. Had Lieutenant Johnson been white, he might have protested further. But Lieutenant Johnson was black, and Dr. Barak felt that a protest might be

83

misinterpreted as a white-black confrontation—the white man defending his institution against the black man's suspicions. Of course he agreed with blacks being given every opportunity for advancement. He had always held that view. On the other hand there was a certain hostility among the blacks themselves toward the whites—understandable in view of the social history of the nation. This insistence on narcotics usage at Greenfields was perhaps a symptom of that hostility. So he said nothing and Lieutenant Johnson, looking at Dr. Barak's big pasty face, his great beak of a nose, and his keen, recessed eyes, reflected that not so many years ago he would have been quelled by the whole façade. He doubted now that there was very much behind it.

There was a knock at the door and Barbara came in. Both men rose to greet her and the lieutenant introduced himself, for they had not met before though he had read her statement to Chief Littleton of the Greenfields police when he had been assigned to the case.

"There're a few things in your statement I want to go over with you," he said. "If you want to talk to me alone, we can go somewhere else. I thought maybe you'd sooner have someone else here."

"I don't mind," said Barbara.

"Okay," said the lieutenant. "There's nothing formal about this. I'm just looking for information—trying to tidy things up. You had a quarrel with Susan Hatfield on the day before she died. In fact you hit her. Why?"

"I can't really explain," said Barbara. "She was rude. She just made me mad. Then Mrs. Venables seemed to have the idea that since Susan was so very clever, she couldn't be wrong. So everything was my fault. It made me mad. It was so frustrating. So I went right upstairs and hit her."

"Do you often lose your temper?" asked the lieutenant.

"No," said Barbara. "Not like that. I can't remember ever having hit anyone before—certainly not a stranger."

"So there was something about Susan Hatfield that made you react in this way—something you hadn't met in other people?"

Barbara considered this before replying. "I don't know whether it was entirely Susan," she said. "It may have been Mrs. Venables, too. She was so—so smug about it. Susan was clever, so Susan was right. And I was just a little dummy. I was to be put with my own kind, who were not bright and clever like Susan. That was part of it."

"When you got back to bed," said the lieutenant, "You said that Susan Hatfield was already in bed. That would have been a little after ten o'clock."

"Yes."

"How do you know she was already in bed?"

"I saw her."

"How could you see her—it was dark?"

"I saw the shape of her feet under the bedclothes in the light from the corridor."

"But you didn't see her face?"

"No."

"So that could have been somebody else other than Susan Hatfield?"

"But why should it be somebody else?" asked Barbara.

"Because Susan Hatfield had a date with the poet, Kenneth Kestion," said Lieutenant Johnson. "Or he says she had. And she maybe needed an alibi for the ten o'clock curfew."

"Susan was a senior," said Dr. Barak. "She didn't need that kind of an alibi. No questions would be asked if she was out an hour or so late."

"Well," said Lieutenant Johnson, "looking over what Miss Minardi told Chief Littleton in her statement, it seems to me that Susan Hatfield didn't want anybody with her in the room that night, and made herself about as nasty as she could to get Miss Minardi to leave. That's what it looks like to me. And yet you say that there was somebody in that bed. So failing to get you to leave the room, so as not to be able to testify that she wasn't there, she then had to get someone to occupy her bed. In other words, it was important for Susan Hatfield, on the night she was murdered, to establish that she was in her room."

"That would suggest that she was up to something—well, illegal," said Dr. Barak. "I can't believe that of Susan. She was such a bright girl."

Lieutenant Johnson sighed. He was beginning to get a little weary of the inevitable phrase. He was beginning to wonder whether Susan Hatfield really was that bright, or whether there was just a consensus on the subject, each member of the faculty hypnotizing the other into the same belief.

"Maybe you can't believe it," said the lieutenant, "but could you have believed that she would have wound up beaten to death in the rose garden?" He turned to Barbara again.

"When did you see Susan last—that is, before you saw her, or thought you saw her, in bed?"

"Just after the lecture that poet gave. She was standing by him. Lots of people saw her."

"Susan had been assigned to play host to Mr. Kestion on

behalf of the student body," said Dr. Barak.

"That would have been about nine o'clock?"

"I suppose so," said Barbara.

"And what did you do between nine o'clock and when you returned to your room?"

"I wandered around the campus," said Barbara.

"Did you talk to anybody?"

"I spoke to Sister Mary McCarthy."

"Anybody else?"

"Nobody that I knew," said Barbara.

"You met someone you didn't know?"

"Yes."

"Where?"

"In the rose garden."

Dr. Barak and Lieutenant Johnson exchanged glances, and Barbara experienced a flicker of fear because of that look.

"Who did you meet there?" asked the lieutenant.

"A boy. A man. He said his name was Jerry."

"Jerry what?"

"Just Jerry."

"What did he look like?"

"I don't know. He was wearing a hat with a big brim and I couldn't see his face."

"Was he tall or short?"

"Tall."

"What happened?"

"We talked."

"About what?"

"Just things. His birthday. My birthday. About nothing, really."

"And nothing else happened?"

"Nothing."

"You saw nobody else in the rose garden?"

"Nobody."

"Have you seen this Jerry since then?"

"No."

"He was wearing a brimmed hat and you couldn't see his face?"

"Yes."

"So even if you did see him, you couldn't recognize him?"

"No. Except I would know his voice. He had a Southern accent."

"Are you sure there ever was a Jerry?"

The question was put softly—almost confidentially.

"Of course I'm sure."

"And this was somewhere between nine and ten o'clock on that evening?"

"Yes."

"You spoke to the nun first—or afterwards?"

"First."

"So suppose you were five minutes talking to the nun and it takes—let's say fifteen minutes to get from the chapel where the lecture was given to the rose garden, you would have got there around nine-thirty?"

"I suppose so," said Barbara. "I was walking slowly. I wasn't really conscious of where I was going. I just went through that hedge and found myself in the rose garden."

"Why didn't you say anything about this Jerry before— why didn't you mention it in your statement to Chief Little-ton?"

"Because it hadn't anything to do with Susan Hatfield

being killed," said Barbara. "It happened before she was killed."

"How do you know?"

"Because she was in bed when I got back."

The lieutenant shook his head. "Kestion says he was with her but let her off in some orange orchard near the campus a little after ten. The coroner says that Susan Hatfield was killed somewhere between nine-thirty and eleven that night. You admit to having been in the rose garden with this Jerry until close to ten o'clock, and we only have your word for it that there was someone in Susan Hatfield's bed that night. That's very odd. That's really very odd."

It was a few moments before Barbara understood the full significance of that remark. Then she said, "I want to talk to my father," and burst into tears.

Twelve

LIEUTENANT MINARDI had been through the total roll of students registered at Greenfields, name by name, without coming upon a single person who answered to the description of Jerry. There were five students with the Christian name of Gerald, but they were all of medium height or less than medium height and when they were run down, their voices did not even approximate that of the student Barbara had met in the rose garden. There were over a hundred students with a middle initial J or G, and these were being checked out but with little hope of success. Of course people often had nicknames that had no relationship to their given name. Then again Jerry need not be a student at Greenfields, though the lieutenant believed he was, for he knew his way about the campus. He was either a student or a former student. But he remained a mystery.

"Don't worry. It's like a knot," he told Barbara. "You keep trying one place and then another place, pulling and pushing and finally you find the right place and it all comes to pieces. Are you sure you don't want to go back to Los Angeles?"

"No," said Barbara. "I want to stay here. I think I'm one of the pieces that has to be pushed and pulled. It all seems to happen around me. There's that funny note that I got. And then the person getting into the goldfish pond in the rose garden that night."

"The note came from that Jerry person, whoever he is," said Minardi. "It's deliberately mysterious and pretty juvenile. We have to find Jerry and not bother with his little games. You're the only person who can find him, because nobody else can recognize him. If you should meet him again and you are alone, you get help right away."

"But, Daddy, I'm sure he wouldn't hurt anyone," said Barbara. "He wasn't that kind of a person."

"They never are," said her father. "But mark what I say. If you recognize him, get help right away. Don't go anywhere alone with him. Don't trust him."

"But, Daddy . . ." said Barbara.

"Barbara," said Minardi patiently. "You're very innocent, and innocent people only see innocence. But I've been a long time on the police force. And innocence not only won't protect you, it is a danger to you. So don't trust people. There's one thing about that note. It was written on the kind of stationery sold at the students' store here. And we have three different fingerprints on it —and something else."

"What else?"

"The footprints of a cat—a cat with black fur."

"I didn't see any footprints," said Barbara.

"You didn't see any fingerprints either," said her father.

"Have you identified them?"

"No. I turned it over to Lieutenant Johnson. But one

kind will be yours, obviously, one probably the person who sold the stationery, and the other Jerry. You should have told Lieutenant Johnson about that note and about the man in the goldfish pond."

"I was frightened," said Barbara.

"I know," said Minardi. "I think he understands that. He knows now anyway." He hesitated and added, "Naturally he's suspicious of you, and so he is not telling me more than he has to. That's understandable. But it makes it difficult for me to do much good. You see, it would be natural for me, in his view, to destroy evidence that might incriminate you. So he doesn't tell me anything and doesn't like me doing any investigation on my own. I'm going ahead. Whatever I find, I'm telling. But I can't expect him to be as open with me. I still wish you'd go back to Los Angeles."

"If I did," said Barbara, "who would recognize Jerry?"

"We'll just keep pulling pieces of the knot and we'll eventually get to him," said Minardi. "Father Bredder thinks it's dangerous for you here, and so do I. I think it's dangerous because you were in the rose garden and spoke with this Jerry. In view of what happened in the rose garden that night, you might be an incriminating witness."

"But, Daddy," said Barbara. "Nothing happened while I was there. Nothing at all."

"No," said Minardi. "But Jerry was pretty anxious for you to go back to your room, wasn't he?"

"He was just being kind," said Barbara.

"That's your view. Mine is he wanted you out of the rose garden."

"Why would he want me out of the rose garden?"

"You answer that," said Minardi. "There's something odd

about that place. You stay away from there. If you won't go back to Los Angeles, why won't you come and stay in the motel with me?"

"Daddy, this is my first time at college and I want to really be in it," said Barbara. "I like being in Hatton Hall and having a lounge of our own, and all of that. And it's only for another week. Nothing is going to happen to me—particularly when everybody knows that you are here in Greenfields."

"Okay," said Minardi. He was going to warn her again to stay out of the rose garden, but he didn't.

Minardi wasn't being quite truthful when he told Barbara he was turning over all he knew to Lieutenant Johnson. He had not told Lieutentant Johnson of the curious coincidence that Edward Smith, drug addict, drowned off a fishing boat, had been from Greenfields, a town with no narcotics record. He didn't tell Johnson, because this was in any case something that should come to Johnson's attention, or at least the attention of the Sheriff's Department, in the normal course of events. And also this was just one lead he wanted to follow up himself. As a policeman he was a little suspicious that there had been no narcotics arrests in Greenfields in four or five years. There was something odd about that, although Greenfields, of course, had its own police department independent entirely of the sheriff's office.

When he had finished talking to Barbara, Minardi returned to his motel and changed his clothes. He changed into a pair of blotched blue pants, cut with the flaring bottoms which were in style, and a green shirt with a flowered yoke about his neck. He put on a pair of jumbo glasses with blue lenses, discarded his socks and instead of shoes wore sandals with uppers of straw and the bottoms made of factory belting. They had cost him ten dollars at Monica's Boutique adjacent to Park La Brea Towers. He put a pack of cigarettes in his pocket, having first of all crumpled the packet, and then put the cigarettes back again. He examined his nails, frowned because they were too short, but put some of the blacking from his shoes under them.

He left his wallet in the motel, took out some single dollar bills which were somewhat soiled and two crisp one hundred dollar bills specially obtained from the bank. He put some kitchen matches in his pocket and a cylinder of lead four inches long and half an inch in diameter. It was his own form of knuckle duster and he took it with him when he was unarmed.

Then he wrote a note to Father Bredder, who was sharing the room with him. It said, "Gone to the café. Back at seven." Father Bredder, he judged, would guess that he meant the Green Bay Tree Café where Smith had worked. Others coming on the note would think he meant the café attached to the motel.

The Green Bay Tree Café lay on the outskirts of Greenfields, beside a two-way highway now little used since it was but two hundred yards from a newer, four-lane highway which ran in the same direction. The two-lane road had not been paved for some time and had many bumps and potholes in it. The particular suburb served by the road had once been an independent hamlet called Mariposa, a word which Minardi recalled with uncertainty was Spanish for butterfly.

There was, a little way down the road, a run-down service station, an agency of the Pelican Oil Company. Its battered sign, hung from a tottering pole, was thick with dust and groaned on rusty hinges in the wind. Beside the service station was a vast barn, the red wash which had once covered its weathered boards still showing here and there, and visible on the vast roof an arrow pointing in the direction of San Bernardino for the benefit of pioneer airmen.

Weeds grew high along the foot of the barn and a peculiar form of climbing grass had worked its way up through the boards and showed in tufts here and there all the way up to the sagging roof. There were a few houses strung along the street—battered, unpainted, and with façades of an ugly yellow brick popular as a building material in California forty years before.

One or two Mexican children were playing in the road and Minardi guessed that the sole present inhabitants of Mariposa were Mexican farm workers, employed in the neighboring orange groves. Behind the hamlet, on the side furthest from the four-lane highway, the lines of the Southern Pacific Railroad passed on an enbankment. In the old days a freight train might stop at Mariposa on request to load oranges. Maybe one still did, Minardi speculated, although the groves about looked poor. The price of picking the fruit coupled with the uncertainty of the labor supply made oranges a chancy crop in California these days.

Minardi had rented a car in Greenfields rather than use his own to visit the Green Bay Tree Café. He reasoned that his own car had been seen outside the Sheriff's Department in San Bernardino and the police station in Greenfields. He pulled onto a strip of dusty parking area before the café, switched off the engine, and stopped before a notice in the dark window which said, "Cafe closed." The notice was handwritten and fairly new. He tried the door anyway, but it was locked. He went around to the back, to the kitchen area, found another door and tried the handle. It was locked, too. He knocked, got no reply, and then called out, "For cripes' sake, somebody open up. Come on. Open up."

He rattled the door vigorously as if in a frenzy and heard someone moving inside. "Who the hell's there?" asked the voice. "We're closed. Can't you read the sign?"

"Open up, wise guy," said Minardi. "You think I come out here for one of your lousy hamburgers?"

"Who the hell is it?" asked the voice.

"Well, it ain't Eddie Smith," said Minardi. "So open the door and find out, like I say."

The door was opened by a heavy-set man whose vast belly, contained in a grayish T-shirt, poured over his waistband in an elephantine roll of fat.

"Who are you?" he asked, blocking the door with his frame.

"Let's just say I'm a friend of Eddie Smith," said Minardi. "I came to get his hits. Where is it?"

"How do I know you're a friend of his?" asked the other. "You don't," said Minardi. He reached in his pocket and took out one of the crisp hundred dollar bills. He made sure his hand trembled a little as he showed it to the man. "Good enough?" he asked.

The man looked from the hundred dollar bill up to Minardi's face. "You want to take off them shades?" he asked.

"No," said Minardi, "the goddam light kills me. It's just like I got fireworks in my eyeballs."

"Okay," said the man and let Minardi in. When the detective was inside, the man stepped out into the driveway and looked about. He walked out to Minardi's car, inspected it, looked up and down the road and came on back.

"Eddie Smith ain't here any more," he said.

"Lincoln's dead, too," said Minardi. "I tell you I've come to get his hits."

"He didn't have any acid," said the man. "Just some clothes. The cops took it."

"Come on," said Minardi. "Quit stalling. I got two bills. Now let me have it. I need it bad, man. I'm about to blow. I gotta get me a fix quick."

"Stay here," said the fat man and waddled out through the narrow door which might at one time have led to a storage shed, for it was a foot less than normal height and so narrow he had to ease his way past. Minardi was left alone in the kitchen. There was a worktable in the center and an old gas-fired range along one wall. A huge refrigerator stood in one corner. He opened it and found it utterly empty. No sheleves in it, but it had perhaps been used for storage of hamburger patties, steaks and bowls of pancake mix and cartons of milk.

It was scrupulously clean. He closed the refrigerator door and turned to an old menu pinned to the left of the range where the cook could see it. It was handwritten in purple ink, the same doleful listing of hamburgers, hotdogs and sandwiches to be found in a thousand such cafés throughout the country. The fat man shouted, "You wanna come in here?" and Minardi stepped through the narrow door to find a flight of steps leading down to a cellar.

"Turn left when you get to the bottom," said the fat man. The detective continued on down and, finding himself in a narrow corridor at the bottom, turned to his left.

Then the whole world disappeared in an explosion of red and gold lights which ended in utter blackness.

Father Bredder returned to the motel from a visit to the rose garden in which he had spent the greater part of the afternoon, found Minardi's note, and when the detective had not returned by six, drove out to the Green Bay Tree Café. He used Minardi's car, for the reason that there was no other transportation available, and got almost hopelessly lost in getting to Mariposa, getting by mistake on the four-lane highway and finding that there was no exit for Mariposa until he had made a U-turn and driven back a mile past the little hamlet. Then he missed the small old road leading to Mariposa, instead taking a road which led him across a bridge over the railway track. He stopped on the bridge to get his whereabouts and could see the little hamlet, or what he supposed was the hamlet, half a mile away, with the old road leading through it.

He followed the line of the railway track with his eyes for a moment, and saw what looked like a bundle tossed onto the tracks. The tracks on the side of the bridge, away from the hamlet, made a slow curve around the edge of an orange grove. A distant rumble, scarcely perceptible above the noise of the traffic on the four-lane highway, announced the approach of a freight train.

Odd that anybody should leave a sack on a railroad track, Father Bredder mused. And then the sack moved very slightly and Father Bredder sprinted off the bridge to where the road met the enbankment, scrambled through a fence of barbed wire, slid down the embankment and ran along the sleepers as hard as he could go. He could see, as he got nearer, that the bundle wasn't a sack but a man with his head wrapped up in a tattered brown jacket.

He could feel the roadbed and the sleepers tremble beneath his feet and heard the urgent wail of the locomotive's whistle. He reached the man and flung him aside and fell after him. With a burst of warm air and the smell of hot diesel oil, the locomotive swept by and came to a shuddering, grinding, screeching stop a hundred yards further on.

Minardi was scarcely breathing. His eyes were open and glazed, but he was unconscious. The engineer leaped from the train and came running back to where the priest was huddled over the bundle. The engineer looked at the detective's pale face and upturned open eyes and said, "Son of a bitch. I could have killed him. That's the second this month."

"What happened to the other?" asked the priest, surprised.

"We scraped him off the wheels with a shovel," said the engineer.

Thirteen

"I LOOKED UP your horoscope," said Father Bredder. "I've gotten to be an expert. You should have stayed in the motel. Your horoscope said you were to avoid any new ventures or contacts with strangers. You should have done nothing."

Minardi, his head in bandages, eyed the priest solemnly. "Looks as though there is a lot more in horoscopes than Mother Church is prepared to admit," he said dryly.

"Your horoscope for today says you are surrounded by friends and good influences. You should do whatever heavy physical work you have been postponing and you will receive a gift from a stranger of the opposite sex."

"How come you are so interested in horoscopes?" asked Minardi.

"It's Kestion's influence," said the priest. "He does everything by horoscope. I am to meet him this evening at nine —not before—and he will have some important news for me. By the way, they never found his clothes."

"His clothes?"

"Yes. He said, you remember, that he drove straight out to Santa Monica and walked into the sea in his clothes. Then he changed on the beach and threw the wet clothes away. The county lifeguards say that they would certainly have turned up by now somewhere between Santa Monica and Malibu. But they haven't."

"It seems a crazy idea to me—to walk into the sea with your clothes on," said Minardi.

"There are a lot of crazy things about his whole case," said Father Bredder. "There's the place that Susan Hatfield was found. I don't just mean the rose garden, but dragged a little way and put under a rosebush which would not conceal her for long. Then there's the man Barbara saw getting into the lily pond—the goldfish pond—in the middle of the rose garden. Why does someone go for a walk in a goldfish pond with their shoes on? Then there's Kestion taking a bath in the Pacific Ocean at night in his clothes. And then there is the attempt to kill you by hitting you over the head and then laying you on a railroad track. That's a very odd murder method."

"Then there's that guy Jerry and his 'Rosy Thoughts,' " added Minardi.

"Before you went to the Green Bay Tree Café," said Father Bredder, "I spent some time in the rose garden. It's horrible to see it now. They've dug up scores of roses and just let them die. They found nothing. They drained the goldfish pond, too, and some of the fish died. They were transferred to a holding tank, but I suppose the shock of being away from their old surroundings killed them. Dr. Barak said that some of those fish were fifty years old according to college legend. They were big. Of course, the students themselves sometimes took a fish for fun, but there are only three big ones left now."

"They were looking for the weapon, I suppose," said Minardi.

"Yes. And anything else they could find."

"Anything in particular?"

"No. Just anything that shouldn't be in a rose garden," said Father Bredder. "I spoke to Lieutenant Johnson of the Sheriff's Department. He's the most active man on the case, you know. Captain Littleton of the Greenfields police has about handed it over to him, and just keeps in touch as a matter of routine. He's a very interesting man."

"Pretty good cop, I'd say," said Minardi.

"He admitted that your being hit over the head removed suspicion from Barbara."

"I wonder what happened to the fat man who slugged me?" said Minardi, changing the subject.

"He's disappeared," said Father Bredder. "I don't think he is very important though."

"I suppose not," said Minardi dryly. "Just that he tried to kill me and he's hooked obviously into the narcotics trade."

"Do you think he hit you—or was there someone with him?"

"I don't know," said Minardi. "It was dark at the bottom of those stairs. The only light—and it wasn't much—came from a room on the left at the end of that corridor. I think I was hit from the right, as I had turned left as he told me. But his voice seemed to come from the left. I walked right into a trap." He sighed. "If there's one rule that holds good in the police business, it is this—never go anywhere alone."

"There was a room on the left in which the fat man lived," said Father Bredder. "It was part of the cellar and a pretty gloomy place. There was a stove in the room—an old iron potbellied stove. And it was full of ashes. Letters—but we could make nothing of them—and a few pieces of wood. We found nothing in the room to identify the fat man."

"What about the people in Mariposa?" asked Minardi.

"Five families," said the priest. "Lieutenant Johnson said they had all been questioned. They knew the fat man by the name of Señor Chili."

"Chili?"

"Yes. Chili. A nickname. Since many of his customers were Mexicans, he served chili with his hamburgers. Whatever his real name was, they didn't know."

"What did he do for fun?"

Father Bredder shrugged. "Went to Mexico—Baja California. Probably Ensenada."

"Well, that would figure," said Minardi. "Ensenada used to be a source of narcotics supply—mostly marijuana, but hard stuff, too, if you knew where to go."

Their talk was interrupted by a nurse who came with a small glass of medicine for Minardi. "You shouldn't be here now," she said to Father Bredder. "I have to ask you to leave." Then, giving the medicine to Minardi, she said, "Drink this."

" 'A gift from a stranger of the opposite sex,' " quoted Minardi, recalling his horoscope as given him by the priest. He swallowed the medicine with a grimace.

Father Bredder next had an appointment, with Dr. Barak. He had been quite open in asking for the appointment, saying that the poet Kestion had asked him to look into the murder of Susan Hatfield in his behalf, and he wanted to talk to Dr. Barak about the case and make his own position about the campus clear. Dr. Barak received him in the same study in the crumbling ivy-covered building in which Barbara had been questioned.

"In a sense I welcome your investigation," said Dr. Barak.

"The presence of the police on the campus is a great disturbance to the students and causes a lot of rumors and gossip. You, working incognito, as it were, may be able to do more good with less—er—upset. You may be sure I will give you all the help I can."

"Thank you," said Father Bredder. "There is one thing I would like to know. The only building overlooking the rose garden is the Theater Arts Building. I have found that there were no activities in that building after eight the night of Susan Hatfield's murder. But I would like to know who has keys to the building. It is just possible that there might have been someone in there who might have seen what happened in the rose garden."

"The distance is considerable," said Dr. Barak. "I doubt anything at all could have been seen by an observer."

"I don't mean that anybody could have been recognized at that distance," said the priest. "But something might have been seen that was important—something that might have appeared quite innocent then but would have signifiance now."

"Can you suggest what you have in mind?" asked Dr. Barak a trifle warily.

"Well," said Father Bredder, "it would be important if anyone saw a black cat near the rose garden. It would have been visible in the moonlight."

"A black cat?" echoed Dr. Barak.

"Yes," said the priest, and he added with a little smile, "black cats were once thought to be the familiars of witches."

"Witches?" said Dr. Barak. "Are you suggesting witchcraft?"

"It's quite popular now," said Father Bredder mildly.

"Horoscopes are in and so is witchcraft. Los Angeles, as you perhaps know, has an official witch—a white witch, as she is called. Then there are black masses. There was one on television recently—perhaps you saw it?"

"You mean you think this kind of occult nonsense lies behind this dreadful murder?" asked Dr. Barak.

"There is this kind of darkness behind every murder," said Father Bredder. "Murder isn't just an antisocial act. It is a terrible violation of the laws of God." He sensed a coldness, a resistance on the part of Dr. Barak, and concluded softly, "I'm just looking for a black cat. A black cat and a black hat with a very large brim. The sort of hat that might be worn in a stage production of someone playing the part of a cowboy or a Spaniard."

"Well," said Dr. Barak, pulling himself together. "Theater Arts did produce *Carmen* a few weeks ago. But there were no black cats. As for who has access to the building when it is closed, there is of course Mr. Peyton, who heads the department. He has a staff of four and I presume each of these is able to get into the building after hours. Will you have to question all these people?" He seemed anxious.

"That may not be necessary," said Father Bredder. "Who is in charge of the wardrobe?"

"That is something you will have to ask Mr. Peyton. No. Just a moment. I think I have that information." He pressed a button on his desk and his secretary entered. "Could you find me one of the programs for the production of *Carmen*?" he asked. The secretary left but was back in a moment with a program which Dr. Barak looked at.

"The costumes were all made by Mrs. Shepherd—she's the wife of the head of our English Department. Perhaps she could tell you about the hat."

Father Bredder obtained instructions on how to get to the Shepherd home, thanked Dr. Barak and left. He was disappointed with the interview. He had hoped for very much more—some show of enthusiasm and energy on the part of Dr. Barak directed toward the solution of the murder. He had got only a correct, formal, civilized interest in its solution, overlaid by the strong inference that it was more important that the students should not be disturbed and the college should not gain any notoriety. It was seven o'clock now and there wasn't time to see Mrs. Shepherd if he was to keep his appointment with Kestion in Los Angeles. Father Bredder had borrowed Minardi's car, and he headed toward Los Angeles, but his road took him past the police station. On an impulse he stopped and, entering, asked for Chief Littleton.

"He's been away in L.A. all afternoon," the desk sergeant said. "But he'll be in tomorrow."

The drive to Los Angeles occupied a little more than an hour, and Father Bredder had a little while to get something to eat before seeing Kestion. He walked four or five blocks across town from the hotel to the cheaper section of the city, and got a hot dog and a cup of coffee at a little café on Broadway. When he got back to the hotel, it was five minutes past nine, and he felt curiously guilty because Kestion had insisted that he be there at nine sharp to conform with the advice of his horoscope. The priest went up to his suite and rang the bell but got no reply. He rang again without result, tried the door and then descended to the lobby to the house phones. He phoned the room but got no reply.

Then he went to the desk clerk. "Can somebody come with me to Mr. Kestion's room?" he asked. "I have an appointment with him and he does not answer." He produced his identification, but the desk clerk said that Mr. Kestion was very firm about not being disturbed.

"If he doesn't answer, he is either not there or he does not wish to be disturbed," he said.

"His key is not in the letter box behind you," said Father Bredder. "So he is probably in his room. It's important that I see him."

"I am afraid I cannot help you," said the desk clerk. "If Mr. Kestion does not answer his telephone or your knock on his door, that is enough for us. I can leave a message for him if you wish."

"Never mind," said Father Bredder, and took the elevator up to Kestion's floor again. He rang once more and was about to leave when he saw one of the laundry workers passing down the corridor.

"Could you help me?" he asked. "I haven't the key and I'm in a hurry." It wasn't exactly a lie, but it was certainly deceit. However, it worked. The laundry woman bustled with her bunch of keys and opened the door, and Father Bredder entered.

Kestion, in a purple dressing gown, was lying on a sofa in the drawing room. He was dead. His eyes were open and the pupils rolled upward so that only the whites showed. On his chest was a note on a piece of hotel stationery which said, "Have a nice day."

Fourteen

FATHER BREDDER did not like the verdict of suicide at all. He could see at the coroner's inquiry at which he had testified that that was the way the verdict was going to go. The medical evidence was that Kestion had taken a massive dose of an hallucination-producing drug, and he listened very carefully to what the pathologist who had performed the post-mortem had to say on this subject.

"The effect of these drugs is to interfere with what I will call the judgment centers of the brain," he said. "It is thought —and this is theory—that the brain is capable of all kinds of extravagant imaginings which are, however, blocked from entering the conscious mind by what I have referred to as the judgment center. The judgment center decides which of these imaginings are of biological value and are allowed to pass on to the conscious and which are useless and are ruled out.

"Drugs which produce hallucinations impair the working of this center, and so exotic visions, pleasing or terrifying, are passed on to the conscious mind. But the impairment of the function of the judgment center also impairs the signals which that center sends to the various vital organs of the body—signals to the heart to beat, to the chest muscles to expand and contract in breathing, and so on. A massive dose of such a drug, taken with the object of intensifying the visionary experience, may so interfere with the judgment center that the vital organs do not receive the correct messages or stimuli, and the heartbeat, for instance, becomes first erratic and then stops altogether.

"Medicine has very little information about the amount of these drugs which can be taken with safety. Those who use them with impunity are then prepared to gamble their lives for a dream."

"In the case of the deceased," said the coroner, "what was the immediate cause of death?"

"His heart stopped beating," said the pathologist, bringing a titter from the audience, among whom there were a great number of the "hippie" sort. The coroner frowned at them and said, "Did the cessation of the heartbeat arise out of what can be described as natural causes?"

"No," said the pathologist. "The heart was quite healthy —good for another thirty years. The condition of the blood in the heart indicated that the heartbeat had been erratic for some time, but the cause of this erratic beat did not lie in the heart, in my view, but in the brain."

The coroner would have returned a verdict of accidental death but for the note which Father Bredder had found on the body. Added to this was the fact that the poet was found to be insolvent and in fact bankrupt. A representative of his principal publisher testified rather sulkily that the poet's royalties had been garnisheed by the Federal government in an attempt to recover five years of unpaid taxes amounting in total to around $30,000 plus interest. The publisher's representative seemed to regard it as a black mark against the United States that poets had to pay income tax.

So the verdict was one of suicide, but Father Bredder did not agree with it. He would have preferred "Murder."

"For heaven's sake," said Minardi, who had by now been released from the hospital, "how can you say murder in face of the medical evidence of an overdose of drugs? Nobody could open his mouth and keep forcing him to swallow pills."

"That's the second and maybe the third death by the same method," said the priest. "It's a very easy method of killing, provided you are dealing with a drug user. You just give them pills supposed to be of a particular strength but including one—just one—about five times that strength. Then you wait. In a little while, at no predictable time, the man will be dead. And the death cannot be traced to you."

"What do you mean, the second—maybe the third!"

"There was Ed Smith," said the priest. "And there was the unidentified man who was run over by the freight train at Mariposa."

"Oh, for gosh sakes," said Minardi, "he was just a bum, dead drunk, and run over by a train."

"That's a guess, isn't it?" asked the priest.

"Well, it's what Chief Littleton at Greenfields said," replied the detective.

"Not identified?"

"No."

"They would try to identify him by circulating finger-prints?"

"That would be one method."

The conversation took place in Minardi's apartment at Park La Brea Towers. It was evening and the city below and around, its shape merging into the darkness, was beginning to reveal its other presence—a presence of towers and lines of lights in buildings and streets. Father Bredder, standing at the window, meditated for a moment on the two physical selves that even a city had—the day city and the night city —each different and yet both the same entity. Could it be true that one view of anything was always wrong—that truth lay in at least two and maybe a hundred views of things; in fact that the more views taken of any particular subject, the closer the viewer came to the truth about that particular subject? Minardi and Littleton were taking a one-view look at the man who had been run over by the train. He had had no identification, was dressed in shoddy clothing and was then a bum who had maybe passed out on the railroad track or stumbled on the tracks in a stupor in the dark and just stayed there and been killed by a train. Maybe he himself was taking a one-view look at things, too—police and criminals; good and evil, each identifiable at a glance. Was it possible that a second glance might reveal good to be evil or evil to be good?

"Would you be able to find whether the fingerprints of the man killed by the train were ever sent to police headquarters in Los Angeles for identification?" asked the priest suddenly.

"Not Los Angeles," said Minardi. "But to California Identification and Investigation Bureau in Sacramento. Take one phone call and maybe ten minutes—provided somebody is not having a cup of coffee."

"So quick—at this hour?" asked the priest, surprised.

"Father," said Minardi. "There are some telephone numbers that never sleep, as it were, and modern scanning equipment is so quick and so efficient that we can pick a particular needle out of twenty-four haystacks all containing needles."

He picked up the telephone, dialed a number, and then

gave an extension number to the operator. "Minardi, Homicide, Los Angeles," he said. "About two weeks ago a John Doe was found dead on the railroad tracks at a place called Mariposa, near Greenfields. Killed by a train. Yes. Mariposa, San Bernardino County. See if we have run a fingerprint check on him. Yes. Call me back. No, not at the department. At home." And he gave his number.

"Why are we doing this?" he asked the priest.

"There is a saying that things aren't always what they seem," said Father Bredder. "And I think that out of that can be got another saying: things that seem different may be the same."

"Maybe you can get that out of it," said Minardi, "but I certainly couldn't. And I think you ought to forget it, because it is leading you astray. You have dug up four deaths —all different. And you say that they're the same; in short, murder. Your attempts to justify this so far don't make much sense to me."

"I know," said Father Bredder. "It's my fault. I am not explaining it very well. And that's because it isn't really very clear to me. The deaths are of two different kinds, aren't they? Kestion and Smith both died from drug overdose . . ."

"Hold on," said Minardi. "Smith died of jumping into the sea and drowning."

"He had had a massive dose of drugs, though," said the priest. "There was some speculation that the drug dose would have killed him anyway, whether he jumped into the sea or not. There was some doubt as to the actual cause of death and I think it was agreed to call it massive shock."

"Okay," said Minardi. "I'll let that go."

"Well, the unknown man on the railroad track and Susan

Hatfield died quite differently. They died by force—one by being run over by a train and the other by being beaten to death with some kind of club."

"All right," said Minardi. "And going along with your saying that things that seem different may be the same, what do you find similar in these four deaths?"

Just then the telephone rang and Minardi picked it up, listened, grunted and put the receiver down. "Those fingerprints were never passed to the C.I.I. for checking," he said.

"They couldn't have been overlooked?" asked Father Bredder.

"No," said Minardi. "Not at our end. Of course policing in a small town is different from policing in a big city, and Littleton may have been a little lax in transmitting them. Small-town police chiefs tend to regard the members of their community as important and drifters and strangers as unimportant. The view has its virtues," he added. "But it falls down when cooperation with other police departments is needed."

Father Bredder was still at the window staring at the city which had now utterly changed. A massive insurance building adjacent, thirty stories or more high, had become a square tower of lights, each light itself square and reaching up into the night sky, utterly different and yet the same thing. The difference lay in the appearance only. Someone who had seen the building only by day would never recognize it by night.

Minardi looked at the figure of the big priest staring out into the night and said, "You think Ed Smith was murdered?"

"No," said Father Bredder, "I think that was an accident."

"Well, that's something," said Minardi. "But you think the unidentified bum and Kenneth Kestion were murdered?"

"Yes, I do."

"Okay. Do you know who the murderer is?"

Before replying, Father Bredder took another long look at the insurance building.

"Yes," he said. "I think I do. But I can't prove it yet, so I won't say anything to you. First I have to find a black hat and a black cat."

Fifteen

THE SONG QUEEN seminar had closed now and the Catholic
girls had won a second prize in one of the contests and been
roundly cheered.

"You suddenly seem to have come to life," said Miss
Princey, the chief instructor. "I am glad that at last we were
able to get through to you girls. You were so stiff when you
came here. What happened?"

"It was Sister Mary McCarthy and St. Augustine who did
it," said Maria.

"Huh?"

"Yes, I asked Sister Mary McCarthy whether it was a sin
to wriggle so much and she said that St. Augustine said that
sin was a matter of intent, and so immodesty was what was
in your mind and not really what you did. Of course we knew
that anyway, but nobody had ever pointed out that it applied
to song queens. So we did much better."

"St. Augustine," said Miss Princey. "Didn't he die ages
ago?"

"In six hundred and four," said Barbara, who had looked
it up, "but, of course, he is still around. That's the nice thing
about saints. There are masses of them and they will all help
you if you just ask."

Miss Princey smiled at the naïveté of the girls and murmured, "Well, it worked." When she was walking away, she had a momentary picture of a robed and bearded figure in a miter hat watching with approval a group of Catholic girls doing high kicks on the lawn of a Baptist college. She put the vision aside, however, as being of no practical use whatever.

Maria now returned to Los Angeles, but Barbara, determined to have her money's worth, reported to the Theater Arts Building and Mr. Peyton for her course in Stage Decoration. The building was fabulously equipped, for Ernst Hochel, who wrote the lyrics and music for the Broadway hit *Next Time, Duck*, had turned over all his royalties to the college in consideration of their having given him an honorary Doctor of Letters degree. It evolved he had never been to high school, having graduated from a Harlem grade school and gone immediately to work in that vast university which is called New York City. Having made a fortune with a grade-school education, he was touchingly grateful for the honorary degree from Greenfields, which was the only college which had thought to honor him.

Barbara had caught but glimpses of Mr. Peyton before, being so very busy with the song queen seminar. He proved to be a tall, well-made young man with a whimsical sense of humor, who had named his study, rather obviously, "Peyton's Place." He held the introductory hour of his seminar in his study, which was vast and decorated in pale blue and ivory, the carpet pale blue, the walls ivory, the ceiling blue and the furniture ivory. He demonstrated his contempt for the conventions by sitting on his desk like a guru and beaming around at the class, themselves seated on chairs or on the floor.

116

"This is quite an uncomfortable position," he said, "but I adopt it to get your attention and to demonstrate the fact that attention is attained by the unexpected—not by the normal. This is so obvious that everybody ignores it, and the few who remain aware of it follow successful careers in advertising, letters, the arts and nowadays even in the sciences.

"Of course, you have to decide in stage decoration, in writing, in painting—in whatever you are doing—whether you *want* to direct attention to a particular area or whether you do not. If you don't want to direct attention to any given area, then you make it ordinary, and it is wrong to make it extraordinary, for you defeat your own purpose.

"Would somebody like to suggest as an example a stage setting for, let us say, a ballerina performing a dance depicting the coming of spring?"

There were many suggestions involving the lavish use of flowered landscapes, trellises, even lambs and shepherds. Mr. Peyton waved them all aside. "Wrong," he pronounced. "You are all certainly in need of instruction. Let's think about this. Spring comes to a land without spring—doesn't it? When we are aware of spring, we are aware of utterly barren trees, of dead branches, of grass brown with winter —and one minute tiny sticky bud on the end of a twig.

"So the ballerina should have an utterly dead stage—all funeral colors. But she should be as gay as a flower and come in under a bright spot and then if she can really dance and express joy and resurrection, you have a tremendous stage setting and a tremendous act. Flowered trellises, backgrounds dripping with wisteria only distract attention from the dancer, who becomes, then, not spring, but a young girl gone slightly mad in an impossible garden."

Not everybody liked this, but they were all fascinated by it, to Mr. Peyton's evident enjoyment.

"One of the things we have to remember in stage decoration—in any aspect of art, for you must remember that all aspects of art are merely slices through the same mountain —is that everything is displayed against the background of our present times and we are so used to that background that if we reproduce it exactly on any stage, we get not a dramatic effect but an effect so ordinary that people feel cheated.

"Reality, exact reality, by the very fact that it is real, is not art at all and has no place in art. If, as a backdrop, you produce a New York skyline exactly as a New York skyline is—with the Chrysler Building and the RCA Building all recognizable—nobody is going to even notice it after the first glance. But if the Chrysler Building looks as if it is in mortal combat with the RCA Building, and if the soaring skyscrapers look as if they are not static but are roaring up toward outer space, then you have New York, for that is what New York is—it is combat and conquest, it is venture, challenge, noise and movement. New York is an entity, the collective mind of man expressed in an art form called a city —an art form which is never at rest. The art form is so overpowering that those who live in New York have constantly to hide from it in apartments as muted and as motionless as tombs.

"All right. We have established that you compel attention by the remarkable, and that you avoid attention by the real or ordinary. Now I can get out of this most uncomfortable posture and discuss a few basics.

"First we have the matter of colors. Color, which used at one time to be sacred—purple was reserved for emperors, as you know, red for kings and cardinals, and white for priests and priestesses—color is now so commonplace that we in the theater are deprived of a most useful tool or stimulant of the mind. We cannot use color as Wagner did in his operas. . . ."

He went on and on, and Barbara listened, fascinated. Here, she decided, was the most brilliant man she had ever met. However ordinary the subject, he filled it with a light of its own, so that instead of being dull, it shone with its own particular glory. He reminded her of Jerry, though his voice was quite different—almost English. He talked about the qualities of colors, some having a sense of fulfillment and others of anxiety, while others were neutral.

"And of all colors," he concluded, "darkness, a no-color, is the most important because whatever relieves darkness is dramatic—whether it is relieved by the appearance of a stain of color or a rustle of sound. Any relief of darkness is intensely dramatic, and I am sure you can all tell me why."

None of them could, so Mr. Peyton explained it himself. "Darkness is death," he said. "There can be nothing more dramatic than that which disturbs death. For that which disturbs death is resurrection—life itself."

After this introduction, the students were divided into groups, each under a different instructor, to investigate various aspects of stage decoration. Barbara's instructor was an older man with a plodding mind which contrasted painfully with that of Mr. Peyton. He took them to a classroom at one end of which was a small stage, and began an exceedingly ordinary talk on the uses of stage space. It was rather like a lesson in geometry by someone who knew all the theorems but had never understood the subject. Barbara was glad for a break of twenty minutes before assembling in the main

119

theater in the building for the next lecture.

Although the seminar was to last only four days, it was to culminate in the arranging of half a dozen stage settings assigned one to each group of students. When they were not at lectures or demonstrations, then the students were expected to get together and work out these settings, starting with sketches and finally collecting all the props and putting them on a stage assigned to them. Barbara's group had been assigned a scene from a play by James Barrie called *Dear Brutus*. The scene depicted a dining room and beyond it French windows opening on a magical garden.

"How can you be original about that?" demanded one of the students. "A garden is a garden is a garden."

"Like a rose is a rose is a rose," said another.

"We could put the trees and flowers upside down," said a third. "That would make it kind of magical."

"How about a scrim with a picture of a garden showing on it by back projection?"

"What's a scrim?"

"Oh, it's just a gauze curtain, but maybe it wouldn't work because too much goes through."

It was agreed that they would think about the scrim and back projection, but they should also look over the flats and backdrops available already, and Barbara was assigned to inspect these and note any that might be of use. She thought she might have to struggle with huge canvases, but this was not so. Theater Arts had its own library, of course, and in the library was a book with color photographs providing an index of all the flats available for use, so she had only to go through this and pick out, by number, any that looked useful.

She did this at the end of the day. The book of photographs

was enchanting, containing the pictures of all kinds of lovely landscapes (there was another one for housefronts and another for streets), and Barbara was surprised and a little disturbed to find, right at the end of the book, a picture of the university's own rose garden. The book gave both an identification number and the name of the designer. The designer's name was Edward Peyton. That was remarkable, because it was such a very ordinary flat, not at all in keeping with the imaginative viewpoints of the head of the Arts Department. Barbara felt that flats and backdrops of this kind—rosebushes and little squares with fountains playing into goldfish ponds—must be found in scores of theaters throughout the country. She was curious, however, took the number, and went to the basement where the flats themselves were stored.

It was near time for the department to close down and the janitor was not on duty or, if on duty, not around. But the flat was easy to locate, for they were all filed according to number. It proved to be large but fairly light, being of canvas and lathes, and Barbara had no difficulty pulling it out of the rack to look at it. As the picture had shown, it was a very ordinary scene. There were large red, white, and pink roses on bushes, and the fountain and the area depicted was that in which the body of Susan Hatfield had been found.

Then Barbara noticed something odd about the roses, something that made them not entirely roselike. She had to examine them closely one by one to find out what the addition was. When she found out, she was frightened. In every rose, embodied in the lines made by the overlapping of the petals, was the suggestion of a death's-head. Some were face on, and right way up. Some were upside down. Some were there in profile. But every rose contained hidden in it, like in the picture puzzles of her childhood, a skull.

While she stared at the picture, something brushed against the back of her legs—something softly and coolly. She turned quickly and saw a black cat, its back arched in pleasure and its tail erect. And then she ran out of the basement and out of the Theater Arts Building. She knew who Jerry was, and she was going to call for help.

Sixteen

LIEUTENANT JOHNSON was not in when Barbara called. He had just left the sheriff's office and nobody knew where he was. Could she leave a message for him? Barbara contented herself with asking that if the lieutenant came back, would he call her at Hatton Hall.

She had calmed down a little and began to wonder whether she was not really jumping at a very big conclusion. All she had found really, was a strange flat painted by Mr. Peyton with death's-heads worked into the roses, and a black cat in the basement of the Theater Arts Building. But a black cat was associated with the strange note she had received with all the quotations about roses. The roses in the garden were associated with the death of Susan Hatfield, for she had died among them. The flat had death's-heads on the roses, as if whoever designed it had had Susan Hatfield's murder in mind. And Jerry was associated with roses, and her father believed that Jerry had written her the note about the roses.

Here Barbara stumbled. What about Jerry's voice? That was the one thing by which she was sure she would recognize him. But Mr. Peyton's voice was quite different from Jerry's Southern drawl. It was a little while before it occurred to Barbara that Mr. Peyton was probably an accomplished actor. Indeed, he had given a fine dramatic performance in his presentation to the seminar that day. And the words that Jerry had used when she met him in the rose garden fitted the personality of Mr. Peyton. He had said, "We who are but wayfarers in time—exiles for a moment from eternity, which is our home . . ." That was exactly the way Mr. Peyton thought. And then what he had said about poetry, "At the bottom of all poetry . . . there is loss." That was like him again. He had that kind of mind. Suddenly Barbara realized that she had stumbled on what Father Bredder called a spiritual fingerprint.

The telephone rang in the lounge of Hatton Hall and the call was for her. She took it in a booth provided for that purpose.

"Miss Minardi?" said the voice. "This is Captain Littleton of the Greenfields police. I called the Sheriff's Department and they told me you wanted to get hold of Lieutenant Johnson. He's away and won't be back for a day or two. Is there anything I can do for you?"

"I think I found something in the Susan Hatfield case," said Barbara. "That's what I wanted to talk to him about. It's a guess, but I think it's important."

"Good," said Chief Littleton. "Lieutenant Johnson is away on another aspect of that case. Maybe you can tell me about it."

"I'd sooner explain it personally, not on the phone," said Barbara. She felt she needed a face-to-face encounter to give credence to her deduction.

Chief Littleton paused and said, "Your father didn't want too many public contacts between you and the police. I think he's right. I could come to Hatton Hall but that might stir some notice. Why don't you meet me at the main entrance to the college? I'll be in a plain car, a new Buick. You can talk to me there, if you think it's important."

"All right," said Barbara. 'I'll be there in about fifteen minutes." She went up to her room to put on a pair of shoes more suitable for walking, for the main entrance to the campus was half a mile away. On her way out she met Sister Mary McCarthy. "I have to go out for a little while," she said, "and I may be back a little late. Will that be all right?"

"Where are you going, dear?" asked the sister.

"I have to meet Captain Littleton. I can't tell you any more than that."

"To the police station?"

"No. I'm meeting him just outside the campus," said Barbara. "But he may want to take me to the police station or to the Sheriff's Department, and that may make me late."

"Is there anything wrong?" There was genuine concern in the nun's voice.

"No. It is just something I want to tell him."

"All right, dear," said the sister. "I won't worry about you then."

The police chief had drawn his car inconspicuously to the side of the road under the shade of one of the massive canyon oaks which formed an avenue leading to the campus gates. He opened the door of the car and Barbara got in.

"I just happened to be back at the station and called the Sheriff's Department on another matter," he said. "Things often happen like that in police work, as I expect your father has told you. I think we ought to drive about so as not to attract attention, and you can tell me what you know while I'm driving." He started the engine, looked carefully about

125

and pulled into the road. "Once I got a ticket from one of my own men for pulling out into the road without looking behind," he said with a chuckle.

"What I have to tell you is a little hard to explain because it depends on—well, not facts, but things that go together," said Barbara. "I told Lieutenant Johnson that the night Susan Hatfield was murdered, I was in the rose garden. It was before ten o'clock, but I don't know the exact time. A man called Jerry came and spoke to me. He was a tall man and wore a broad-brimmed Spanish kind of hat and I couldn't see his face. I never could find Jerry afterwards, and my father couldn't find him either. But I got a note with a lot of things written about roses on it. Quotations and so on. And they found some fingerprints on it and the prints of a cat's paw and some black hair from a cat. So whoever wrote the note had a black cat and could be identified by their fingerprints, too. Only you know about fingerprints. If they are not on file, you can't get any identification. And they're only on file if people have been in trouble before, or if they've had a government job or something like that. I mean lots and lots of fingerprints are not on file."

"That's right," said the chief.

"So the identification between the note and the writer would maybe be traced through the cat. My dad told me to look for a black cat, and I found one. I think it's the only one on the campus. It lives in the basement of the Theater Arts Department."

"That's kind of interesting," said Chief Littleton. "Got anything else?"

"Yes," said Barbara, encouraged. "I had to go through the painted flats to help make a stage setting and I found one of

126

the rose garden—the same rose garden Susan Hatfield was murdered in."

"Well," said Littleton dubiously, "I guess if they needed a scene of a rose garden, that would be a good one to paint."

"I know," said Barbara. "But this wasn't just a painting of a rose garden. All the roses have skulls hidden in them. Like puzzle pictures. And the scene centers on the part of the rose garden where Susan Hatfield was murdered. The flat was painted by Mr. Peyton, who is head of Theater Arts, and he's a very good actor. And I think he's Jerry."

Littleton drove in silence for a while, thinking deeply. The car was traveling down the four-lane highway which paralleled the only road leading to Mariposa. He slowed and pulled off the highway onto the old road.

"Where are we going?" asked Barbara.

"I'm going to look over that place your dad got into trouble looking at," he said. "I've got a hunch that I might find something there related to what you just told me. You can stay in the car if you want. I just want to take a quick unexpected look through."

He pulled the car up in front of the Green Bay Tree Café, whose windows were still dark and still displayed a "Closed" sign. It was now dusk and two or three children were playing in the street further down the road. They paid no attention to the car as it pulled up other than to give it a glance. A fat man waddled out of a house, looked at the car, and waddled back in again. The chief had gone into the café by the back entrance. Barbara was concerned about the fat man. He resembled the Señor Chili who had run the café, the man who had beaten her father and put him on the railroad track to be run over by a train. She noted the house he had gone into and slipped out of the car to get Chief Littleton. She found him in the kitchen of the grubby café.

"Chief," she said excitedly, "there's a fat man in the house down the road. He's very fat. He looks like the man my father said he met here—the man who tried to kill him."

The chief, who had been standing by the door of the big refrigerator, looked at her gravely. "You're either the unluckiest kid I ever met or the most noticing kid I've ever met," he said. He opened the refrigerator door and pulled out his gun. "Get in," he said.

Barbara stared at him in horror. "What do you mean?" she said.

"You know too much," said the chief. "Get in. It won't be bad. You fall asleep and you have a vision. That's the build-up of carbon dioxide, but they say it's like going to heaven. Like taking a little acid. I don't know. I never touch the stuff. Then you die."

Barbara didn't move. The revolver was level with her chest and only a few feet off. "You wouldn't dare shoot," she said. "They'd find you."

"What you're forgetting is that the 'they' you're talking about is me," he said. "Get in."

Trembling, she sat on the floor of the refrigerator's interior. "Get your legs in," said the chief, "or I'll break them in the door." And when she moved them, the door swung shut and she was swallowed in darkness.

Father Bredder had called on Mrs. Shepherd, the wife of the head of the English Department, and she had received him in a huge and lovely garden, so full of iris of every shade, all in bloom, that the priest thought it a corner of heaven.

Mrs. Shepherd loved gardening, and since this was also a favorite pastime of the priest, they got along famously. They talked so much about flowers that it was some time before Father Bredder got around to asking her about hats.

"There were half a dozen black hats made for the *Carmen* production," said Mrs. Shepherd.

"Did you make them?" asked the priest.

"I faked them," said Mrs. Shepherd, smiling. "We got large straw hats—hats with small crowns and big brims like the orange workers use—and covered them with black material. Mr. Peyton was quite fond of them and wore one for a while. He has a child's love of the spectacular."

"He's the head of the Theater Arts Department, isn't he?"

"Yes. Very talented. And thorough. And original. He got a black cat for a Macbeth production—you know the witches on the heath scene. He opened the scene with an utterly dark stage and the sounds of wind and then one spotlight on the cat, high up in one corner of the stage with a broomstick behind it. It was quite exciting."

"It must have been," said Father Bredder. He looked about and said, "The iris are just heavenly."

"When I dig them up in August, I'll send you some rhizomes," said Mrs. Shepherd, and took his address.

Father Bredder thought of going to the Theater Arts Building for an interview with Peyton after leaving Mrs. Shepherd, but the building was now closed and it was more important to see Chief Littleton. He walked to the police station in Greenfields deep in thought, and the walk occupied the better part of an hour. He felt sickened and at the police station he was told the chief had left.

"You don't know where he went?" he asked the sergeant.

"He didn't say."

"Has Lieutenant Johnson been in?"

"Not that I know of. He's with the Sheriff's Department, you know."

"Yes," said the priest. "I wonder could I use the telephone and call him?"

Somewhat grudgingly the sergeant let the priest through the counter over which they were talking and, indicating a telephone, gave him the number.

"Is Lieutenant Johnson there?" said the priest when the connection was made. There was a silence and then Johnson spoke.

"I'm at the Greenfields police station," said the priest. "I wonder if I could see you. I have something important to tell you."

"This must be my day for people saying they have something important to tell me," said Johnson in his rich drawl. "That Minardi girl called me about an hour ago. I wasn't in, but she had something important to tell me."

"Oh," said Father Bredder, "did you reach her?"

"No. I called Hatton Hall on the campus where she's staying, but they told me she had gone out to see Chief Littleton, and might not be back for some time."

"Lieutenant," said Father Bredder, and his voice was full of urgency, "I have to see you right away. It's a matter of life and death. Can you come to the Greenfields police station?"

"Okay," said the lieutenant, and hung up.

"What car was Chief Littleton driving when he left here?" Father Bredder asked the sergeant.

"His own car. It's a new Buick sedan."

"And you're sure you don't know where he went?"

"He didn't say," said the sergeant. "If it's that urgent, I could call him on the police radio. No. Just a moment. He just took delivery of that car—it's his own—and his receiver hasn't been installed yet."

Father Bredder's mind was working fast now, and when Lieutenant Johnson came in, the priest seized him by the arm and rushed him out to his car.

"Drive to the Green Bay Tree Café in Mariposa," he said. "I have a horrible suspicion about that big refrigerator."

Seventeen

BARBARA WAS barely conscious when Father Bredder opened the door of the refrigerator. She had tried to move away part of the rubber seal to get air, and her face was against the door when he pulled it open. He grabbed her as she fell and something slithered to the floor and lay there gleaming. The priest carried her outside and after a little while she revived, opened her eyes, and saw him with enormous relief.

"I prayed so hard," she said, sobbing. "I was so frightened. I didn't want to die. Chief Littleton . . ."

"We know," said the priest. "Don't think about it any more. Everything is going to be all right. It's all over now." He put her head against his ample chest and stroked her hair to soothe her.

"I used my rosary to hold the rubber aside and get some air," said Barbara. "I had it around my neck. It protected me like Sister said. I stuffed it in the hinge and then I said my prayers on my fingers until . . . It was awful!"

"Don't think about it any more," said the priest. "You are safe now and nobody can hurt you any more. I should have warned you about Littleton—but I couldn't be sure."

At that moment Lieutenant Johnson came out of the café

carrying the rosary a little self-consciously. "I found this on the floor, miss," he said, and gave it to her.

"You had better get an all-points sent out for Littleton," said Father Bredder. "He drove her here and tried to kill her because she knew too much."

Johnson looked hard at Barbara and then at Father Bredder. He shook his head in disbelief and went to the patrol car to make the broadcast. Father Bredder left Barbara with the lieutenant and went into the café to look around. There were two entrances to the kitchen—one from the parking area which extended from the front of the café along the side and another opposite, giving access to a small outdoor work area where potatoes could be peeled and where garbage was kept out of sight of the customers. The door to this entrance was ajar, and the priest pondered this for a moment, wondering if the lieutenant had taken a look outside and failed to close the door afterward.

He had searched the café before, after Minardi had been attacked, but it was a search carried out in the presence of Chief Littleton. Now he wanted to go carefully through those ashes in the cast-iron stove in the cellar. He gave another glance at the rear door, slightly opened, and went into the cellar. He went down the steps using a trick he had been taught in the Marines—that is, he started by descending one step, then went back up again and redescended so anybody counting steps below would think he had already come down three steps when he had come down only one. When he got two steps from the bottom, he halted. If there was going to be a blow it would come now, delivered on empty air.

But no blow came and the cellar, it seemed, was deserted.

The ashes, however, were still in the bottom of the cast-iron stove. There was a meager light from two small windows by the top of the wall which were just level with the ground. It was not much light, but it was enough to distinguish burned paper from unburned, and the priest started to carefully sift through the ashes to the very bottom. What had been burned there were letters—letters written on very thin paper whose ashes crumbled at a breath. But under two charred sticks whose ends were touching the bottom of the stove he found a portion of an envelope, scorched but with a foreign stamp still mostly intact.

He examined the stamp and made out the letters Arg - - t - na. Argentina. He put the piece of paper carefully between the pages of a very worn missal which he always had with him, and returned to the lieutenant's car.

"I sent out an all-points and I took a quick look down there for the fat man," said the lieutenant. "But he's gone. Funny sending out that kind of a message. An all-points for a police chief, with the warning that he's armed and should be considered dangerous."

He shook his head, still bemused. "I had it about figured out that Kestion killed that girl," he said. "Never did find his clothes. Blew up my whole case."

"Kestion couldn't have done it," said the priest. "There was no motive."

"With these hopheads you don't need a motive," said Johnson. "They're like wild beasts. They kill when they get mad. And you can't tell when they'll get mad."

Police Chief Littleton drove back to the police station after the all-points bulletin for his arrest on a charge of attempted murder had been broadcast. A repeat of the broadcast was just coming over the station receiver as the chief walked in and he heard the words, "Chief Thomas Littleton of the Greenfields police, height six foot two, weight one hundred and eighty-five pounds, driving a new Buick sedan, License Number TOP Six. . . . This man is armed and must be considered as dangerous."

The sergeant saw the chief coming, but didn't have the presence of mind to cut the loud-speaker. The sergeant reached for his hip before he remembered that, seated at his desk, he had removed his gun belt and holster. The chief pulled out his own revolver and leveled it at the sergeant, and the sergeant sat back down in his chair and looked at him miserably.

"It's no good, Chief," he said. "It's an all-points. You haven't got a chance."

The gun still remained level and the police chief started backing out of the building. He had reached the front door when Johnson pulled up and saw him in the lighted lobby. The chief whirled around, his revolver ready. There were two shots, and the chief stumbled backward as if he had been hit a tremendous blow on the chest. He fell flat on his back so hard that his gun flew up in the air and crashed into the lobby wall. The sergeant at the desk got up, trembling, and walked slowly out of his office and looked down at the body of Chief Littleton. There was a bright red stain on his chest and a very neat hole in the cheekbone below his left eye. He was dead.

The sergeant looked at Lieutenant Johnson coming up the steps with his gun still in his hand and said in a curiously high-pitched voice, "I guess they'll call it police brutality." Then he laughed nervously and wiped the sweat off the back of his neck with his hand.

Eighteen

"THE LESSON is," said Mr. Peyton, "that a man of intellect and talent—since modesty demands I make some qualification—should never associate with a fool. Otherwise the fool will destroy him. That, of course, is the underlying tragedy of Hamlet. Hamlet was a fool, and he succeeded in destroying all the better people around him—his uncle, his mother, Ophelia, Laertes, even Polonius, who isn't quite the bleating sheep that everybody tries to make him out."

Lieutenant Johnson flipped on the switch on the tape recorder and glanced at Minardi and Father Bredder and said, "I have to caution you that anything you say will be recorded and may be held in evidence against you. You have the right to legal counsel at this time and you are not required to answer any questions I put to you, nor are you required to testify against yourself in any particular."

"Fire away," said Peyton. "This may be quite amusing."

"Littleton was using his position as chief of the Greenfields police to operate a narcotics ring here, his major outlet being the Green Bay Tree Café," said Johnson. "That much we know or will know after questioning the people in Mariposa. How did you get associated with him?"

"Through Susan Hatfield," said Peyton. "She was the clod

behind the whole thing. God save me from the scientific mind. There is nothing more turgid, more bigoted, more rigid in its viewpoint than a chemist—and she was a very good chemist. She took a semester with me in Theater Arts, and she was absolutely hopeless. She had no imagination at all. There was nothing inside her skull but that damned logical brain of hers—or if there was, she wouldn't let it out. Artistically she was a zombie. When I spoke to her of imagination, the joys of creative work, the delights of the spirit, the thing we call inspiration, she had to have a scientific explanation for it all. Where does inspiration come from? Where did *Paradise Lost* come from? Susan Hatfield asked herself these questions and her reply was body chemistry. The road to heaven, my dear Father," he said, "is not through the church but through a test tube. A little acid can make mystics and angels of us all."

"I think you are talking about the road to hell," said Father Bredder.

Peyton was wildly annoyed at this. "Have you ever taken any?" he asked. "You shouldn't talk about it until you have, you know. It provides the gateway to another place, a place so amazing that words really cannot describe it. Imagine, however, Himalayas crusted with gems, Niagaras of diamonds tumbling down from a thousand miles in the sky to the symphonies of Beethoven, forests whose trees have transparent leaves in all the colors of stained-glass windows but with a light never seen on earth. Heaven, Father. The gates of heaven. Nothing less. And these opened by Susan Hatfield's clever little test tube. Though she wouldn't touch the stuff herself."

"Why did she make it, then?" asked Minardi, also present at the questioning.

"She started out trying to prove to me that my talents were the result of body chemistry—that in fact I hadn't any talents at all. I was just the result of a chemical reaction. I have my off days, you know, like everybody else. She said that was because I'd run out of the needed chemistry. And on one of my off days, she offered to supply it—and did. The result was tremendous."

He glanced at Father Bredder and said, "The saints of your church knew about body chemistry long before Susan Hatfield, Father," he said. "The mystics and visionaries knew its workings. Read Huxley's *Hell and Heaven*. It is all in that eminently logical little book. The saints used exactly the same method to achieve visions as the chemists, but more painfully. They flogged themselves or starved themselves and so produced the biochemical condition which led to visions. They saw archangels as big as mountains, and the Seventh Heaven, and God Himself. Fasting, you know, not only lowers the efficiency of the inhibiting, reasoning brain by depriving it of vitamins, but it also removes nicotinic acid from the blood. And nicotinic acid is a terrible preventer of visions. So you see, prayer will not get you into Paradise, but lysergic acid will."

"This stuff's all getting on the tape," said Johnson petulantly.

"So it should," said Peyton. "It's what it's all about anyway, as you'll see."

"Where did Littleton come in?" asked Johnson doggedly.

"Susan made the stuff for me," said Peyton. "And I gave it to one or two people who needed help. Not everybody. Just the poor blind bastards who couldn't get their eyes any higher than earthworms. Then Littleton found out, and traced the supply to me. That wasn't hard. But he was amazed to discover that I wasn't selling it, just giving it away. I hadn't the slightest interest in making a penny out of it. And I never have. Visions should not be for sale. I am sure Father Bredder will agree with me there.

"Anyway, to make a shorter tale of these boring details, Littleton told Susan that he would not prosecute provided she supplied him as well. He frightened her with tales of jail and all that rot, though I suppose actually she could have gone to jail. But you know she had a very unhappy childhood —very lonely. She was rejected by her parents, and added to the normal fears anybody has of going to jail was a deeper fear of another rejection—a rejection by society, in which she was making a place for herself. So she agreed to supply Littleton. Then she got frightened."

"What frightened her?" asked Minardi.

"Smith getting high and walking off the fishing boat," said Peyton. "Smith was the contact man between her and Littleton. He worked part time as a gardener on the campus. He picked the stuff up and gave it to Littleton. It was a nasty arrangement that completely disgusted me. Why is it that when you find something to help people with, all these pigs come along and start making money out of it? The only saving grace about that whole business with Littleton was the arrangement for the pickup, and for that I take the credit."

"What was the arrangement?" asked Johnson.

"Well, I suggested that the pickup spot should be the rose garden. I thought it entirely proper, because when we think of heaven we think automatically, by some kind of instinct, of a beautiful garden. What more appropriate place, then, to pick up the key to heaven, as it were, than in a lovely garden?"

"The sunken rose garden?" said Johnson.

"Yes."

"Where in the sunken garden?" asked the lieutenant.

It was Father Bredder who answered. "In the goldfish pond," he said.

"How did you know that?" demanded Peyton, genuinely surprised.

"That was Barbara's contribution," said the priest. "She saw the wet footsteps leading from the pond at night—made by Chief Littleton, who of course had been wearing gun boots to get into the water and searching for some missing capsules of acid. There were quite a few missing."

"I suppose Smith took the missing drugs?" said Minardi.

"Oh, no," said the priest. "I don't think he stole them. He got his supply for his work. It was the goldfish who took them."

"The goldfish?"

"Yes. Some of the goldfish were quite big and could readily swallow a capsule of drugs. The capsules were put in a weighted container in the goldfish pond. The capsules were weighted themselves. But the goldfish worried the container until they got it open and then swallowed some of the capsules. When Smith made his last pickup, some of the capsules were missing. Littleton may have suspected that Smith took them, but Smith insisted he hadn't. Chief Littleton reasoned correctly that the goldfish had got them, and so he went fishing at night."

"Fishing for goldfish at nighttime in a pond?" said John-

140

son. "He wouldn't have much chance of catching them, would he?"

"No. Not fishing for goldfish, but fishing for the capsules," said the priest. "If you ever watched fish feeding in an aquarium, you may have noticed that anything they don't like they eject from their mouths almost immediately. He reasoned that if the fish had taken the capsules they would have ejected them, and they would be lying somehwere in the mud at the bottom of the fishpond near where the container was put. He had to find the capsules before the pond was drained while looking for the murder weapon, which was why he took the risk."

"That's pretty clever of you," said Peyton.

Father Bredder looked at him calmly. "Mr. Peyton," he said, "you have not told us why you made an appointment to meet Susan Hatfield the night she was murdered in the rose garden."

"I didn't have an appointment to meet her," retorted Peyton. "I might point out to you that if I wanted to meet her, I could meet her at any time."

"Then why did you go to the rose garden that night—the particular night that she was killed?" asked the priest. "We know that you did, because you met Barbara Minardi there."

"It was just a whim," said Peyton.

"Wasn't it something more than a whim?" said the priest.

"You were so clever about the goldfish, why don't you tell me why?" said Peyton.

"I will try," said the priest. "But you haven't told us the full story of your relationship with Susan Hatfield. You haven't told us that she was in love with you."

"Dear God," said Peyton, "practically every girl who

141

takes my course falls in love with me. It's part of what they get for their fee, I suppose. It doesn't mean anything. They come from flatlander homes with mothers who save savings stamps and fathers who get boiled every night on beer and television, and anything that in the slightest degree is imaginative and male sweeps them off their feet. I have a dozen students in love with me every semester."

"But not like Susan Hatfield," said Father Bredder. "She had no love in her life, and falling in love with you was probably the most wonderful thing that had happened to her in all her lonely years. You knew that, didn't you, Mr. Peyton?"

Peyton said nothing.

"She didn't decide to stop supplying acid, as you call it, because of the death of Smith," continued the priest. "Smith meant nothing to her. But she was afraid that the poison—for poison it is—would kill you, too. That is why she stopped. Isn't that right?"

"I will admit only that coupled with her fishlike scientific mind she had the most astonishing puritanical ideas," said Peyton.

"Does concern for the safety of people you love—even if they don't love you—strike you as puritanical, really?" asked the priest gently. "Does it, Mr. Peyton?"

"This is all too trite," said Peyton. "You are trying to make an Edwardian love story out of what was, if it was anything, a conflict between the arts and the sciences—myself the arts and that dull girl the sciences."

"The dull girl is dead," said Father Bredder. "She was killed horribly and she died to protect you."

"Oh, come now," said Peyton. "Do you think I was next in line to be battered to death?"

"Yes, you were," said the priest. "Though not in the way you think. But to prevent your soul—or spirit if you wince at the word—being battered to death by lysergic acid, becoming entirely dependent upon chemical stimulation with all its other dangers, she cut off the supply to you and to Chief Littleton. She did so at the risk of her life, for Littleton threatened to prosecute her and jail her for trading in acid in the past if she didn't keep making it for him. And when she told you of these threats, you just laughed and told her to go on making it. You could have helped her, Mr. Peyton. You could have been concerned for her and been a witness for her against Littleton. But you wanted the acid yourself and you have always held yourself far more important than anyone else. You had had a glimpse of hell, thought it heaven, and you wanted more. So you said you would not testify against Littleton. That left her with only one friend she could turn to. Her father."

"Her father?" said Lieutenant Johnson. "She hadn't seen him for years. He is in Argentina."

"He was," said the priest. "He's dead now. Her father was the unidentified down-and-out who was found run over by the freight train at Mariposa."

"How do you know that?" demanded Minardi.

"I don't really know it," said the priest. "And we won't know for sure until the fingerprints of the man are checked against those of Mr. Wallace Hatfield—Susan's father. But I deduce that he was her father, and I think I have some pretty strong evidence."

"Such as?" queried Johnson.

The priest reached in his pocket and took out his worn missal. The black leather of the cover gleamed in his hand as he opened it and took out the scrap of the envelope he had found in the stove of the Green Bay Tree Café.

"Chief Littleton had all of Susan Hatfield's papers," he said. "He got them right after she was murdered. And he burned them in that stove in the café. But this survived—an airmail stamp from Argentina, where her father lived. You can understand, of course, why he burned them. Because he had to destroy any suggestion that she was in touch with her father before her death. Her being in touch with her father was the motive for both her father's death and her own. The weapon that puzzled us was an obvious weapon for a policeman—one that would not put Susan on the defensive—his billy club."

"Anything else?" asked Johnson.

"In Susan Hatfield's pocketbook were a number of airmail stamps," continued the priest. "There were some twenty-one-cent airmail and seventeen-cent airmail. Chief Littleton forgot to get those. The twenty-one-cent stamps would be for European airmail—letters to her mother. The seventeen-cent ones would be South American airmail—letters to her father."

"It still isn't much to go on," said Lieutenant Johnson.

"There's the mutilation death of the unidentified man in the clothing of a down-and-out," said the priest. "When I first heard of it, the engineer told me they had had to scrape the body off the wheels. And when I inquired later by looking up the newspaper accounts, they stated that the features were unrecognizable and speculated that the victim had been drunk or drugged and had become unconscious lying on the railroad track."

Johnson shrugged. "That's what I thought. Could be."

Father Bredder shook his head. "I know down-and-outs,"

he said. "There are a lot of them on Main Street. Many are friends of mine. Their method of travel is 'riding the rods'— which is very often lying on the cross-bracing of the under-carriage of freight cars. They are experts at it. They showed me how to do it once—one night in the Los Angeles freight yard. It is a considerable skill. There's one thing about down-and-outs, though. They are railroad experts. They know the dangers of railroads. They know pretty well how long it takes a train to come to a stop. And so they know that the worst place in the world to pass out is on a railroad line. So when I heard of the death of this man, I knew that he was not a hobo. And when I read that his features were unrecognizable and then discovered that a request for identification had never been sent to the California Identification and Investigation Bureau, I suspected that Chief Littleton wanted to conceal his identity.

"It makes a horrible story. The girl whom you rejected, Mr. Peyton, wrote to her father telling the trouble she was in. He, hoping to atone for his past neglect of her, came back and identified himself to Littleton, with whom he had an appointment at the Green Bay Tree Café. There he was knocked out, stripped of his clothes and identity, put in rags and laid on a railroad line in time for a freight train to cut him to pieces. And that death made the death of the daughter Susan inevitable."

"They'd have to time that pretty well, wouldn't they—to be sure that Hatfield was unconscious long enough for a freight train to arrive and run over him?"

"No," said the priest. "They had a place they could store him and wait for a train. In the refrigerator."

"He would have died in there," said Johnson.

"I hope he did," said the priest quietly.

"Let's get back to the rose garden," said Lieutenant Johnson doggedly. "We know Mr. Peyton was there. He says he was there on a whim. Do you want to stick to that story, Mr. Peyton?"

"No," said Peyton. "I don't. I had a reason for being there." He glanced at Father Bredder and said somewhat sarcastically, "One you probably won't believe."

"What was it?" asked Johnson.

"Susan had told me that Chief Littleton wanted to see her in the rose garden that night," he said. "She said she was frightened of him. She asked if I could be nearby. He had been threatening her, as you said, because his business in narcotics was about to blow up. Do you know something? She was so frightened that she actually showed emotion. Yes, she came close to crying. It was pretty awful. Out of pure embarrassment I said I'd be around to help if need be."

"Out of embarrassment?" asked Father Bredder.

"Well, I felt—oh, all right, I felt sorry for her—just a little bit. But mostly embarrassed. To see that flat, cold, scientific mind breaking up. It wasn't nice."

"Mr. Peyton," said Father Bredder, "that little drop of compassion that you felt may save you yet. It was perhaps the first touch of concern for others to break into your consciousness in all your years of self-adoration. Do not, I beg of you, throw it aside. Recognize what is real—what your soul says is real—for you have lived with what is artificial for so long you are in great danger."

"The tape," said Lieutenant Johnson testily. "This is all getting down on the tape."

Peyton ignored the lieutenant and looked anxiously at

146

Father Bredder. "Do you remember the start of Newman's essay—' "What is Truth?" said jesting Pilate, and stayed not for an answer . . .' "

"Yes," said Father Bredder. "The cynicism of that question made him Pilate, what he was. His sin was the same as yours—he put so little value on truth that in the end he did not care what was true and what was not. Down that road lies damnation."

"Very edifying," said Peyton. But he was shaken by the priest's words.

"You were in the rose garden thinking Susan Hatfield was in danger," said Lieutenant Johnson. "But you met Barbara Minardi there and thought it better to get her out of the way first—is that about it?"

"That is about it," said Peyton. "Susan Hatfield was frightened. She said Littleton had asked that in meeting her she establish an alibi—horrible word that—so that it would appear that she was in bed at the time."

"An alibi for her would actually be an alibi for him," said Minardi. "That is interesting. And an alibi established on the word of the daughter of a policeman would be a pretty good alibi. What happened after you took my daughter to her dormitory?"

"I went back to the rose garden—but I was too late. She was already dead."

"Did you go right back?"

"Yes."

"Did you find her body immediately?"

"Actually no. I was ten or fifteen minutes walking about in the rose garden waiting for her and Littleton to turn up when I found her. I just happened to go down that particular

147

aisle of grass between the roses and saw her."

"Was she dead?" asked Minardi.

Peyton shuddered. "I didn't stop to find out," he said. "I hope she was."

"The realities frighten you, don't they, Mr. Peyton?" said Father Bredder. "Life. Death. You are afraid of them."

"Why did you write that note about roses—'Rosy Thoughts'?" asked Minardi.

"I really don't know why," said Peyton. "I had found out by then who your daughter, whom I had met in the garden, was. And I suspected that the song queen seminar was only a cover up—that she had actually come to Greenfields because some rumor of Susan Hatfield's drug activities had reached the ears of the Los Angeles police."

"The Los Angeles police have no jurisdiction out here," said Minardi.

"Which would be a very good reason for using the daughter of a Los Angeles policeman to investigate," countered Peyton. "You don't think that people are so silly as to think that police investigate things only in their own areas, do you?"

"What were those 'Rosy Thoughts' supposed to convey?" asked Minardi.

"Oh, just stimulate her interest. I felt guilty about the murder of Susan Hatfield. But who was I to tell anyway— Chief Littleton?"

"You could have told me," said Lieutenant Johnson.

"And of course you would have believed me right away," said Peyton sarcastically, "because when a citizen makes a complaint about a policeman to another policeman, the citizen is always believed. Don't be silly. I couldn't tell anybody.

I could only try to get the Minardi girl interested. Get her curious. Because the whole investigation seemed to be pointing to the poet Kestion as the culprit."

"Who told you that?" asked Johnson.

"Chief Littleton,' said Peyton with a smirk. "He didn't know I knew he had been in the garden with Susan, and I wasn't about about to tell him or I would have been clubbed, too—or maybe run over."

"Would it have bothered you if Kestion had been arrested and accused?" asked Father Bredder.

"Yes," said Peyton. "It would have. I am not entirely without a conscience."

"Would you have done anything about it?" asked the priest.

"I don't know," said Peyton. "I don't know. I might have. He was an artist. Artists are special. There is no use pretending they aren't superior. That is a vulgarity called democracy. Artists are superior. Artists are not to be destroyed. They are to be protected. Perhaps I would have done something if Kestion had been accused."

"Mr. Peyton," said Father Bredder, "artists are only artists when their deepest concern is not for themselves but for all mankind. As soon as they think themselves more important than the least of all the creatures on earth, they cease to be artists."

"How would you know?" demanded Peyton. "You are not an artist."

"That is true," said Father Bredder. "But for you and me, Mr. Peyton, the greatest of all artists died on a cross."

In the silence that followed, nobody seemed to be able to think of anything more to say. And then Father Bredder turned to Lieutenant Johnson and asked mildly, "Did Kestion's clothes ever turn up—the clothes he says he dumped in the Pacific Ocean when he went for a midnight bath?"

"Yes," said Johnson. "They did."

"When?" asked the priest.

"I found them myself. I had been away looking for them the day Barbara Minardi called me and got Littleton instead."

"Where did you find them?" asked the priest.

"Paradise Cove."

"That's west of Santa Monica, isn't it?" asked the pirest.

"Yes. Quite a piece."

The priest sighed. "Lieutenant," he said, "you should have stuck to your original plan and never admitted finding those clothes."

"What do you mean?" demanded Johnson.

"The clothes couldn't have been found at Paradise Cove," said the priest. "Although the offshore current goes west, the inshore current, where the clothes would have been thrown off, goes east. You were hand and glove in this with Littleton, and the clothes of a man whom you know was murdered have testified against you out of your own mouth."

Nineteen

THE CASE against Lieutenant Johnson for illegal possession and sale of narcotics and conspiracy to commit murder was not easy to prove and might have failed but for the arrest two months later of the fat man, Señor Chili. He was found by mundane police methods. A police artist drew his picture from Minardi's description, and this was circulated with a photostat of the menu showing his handwriting which Minardi had picked up in the kitchen of the Green Bay Tree Café. A note was made in the circular that Señor Chili was a short-order cook who specialized in highly spiced dishes. That was sufficient. As Minardi remarked, "We are all victims of our habits, and Señor Chili won't be able to stay away from putting out his own menu and making spiced food for long." He served an almost uneatable dish of chili beans to an off-duty police officer, and that was his downfall.

Arrested, he admitted to the name of Pete Croton, and his fingerprints brought a host of aliases to light and a host of offenses from issuing false papers to Mexican migrants to tampering with the mails, and "peonage"—the crime of supplying a man and his family with the bare necessities of living and paying them no wages or keeping what wages they earned if employed by another.

He was now charged with possession and sale of narcotics, complicity in the murder of Susan Hatfield's father, and complicity in the attempted murder of Lieutenant Minardi and Barbara Minardi.

Until the fat man's arrest, the case against Lieutenant Johnson rested on a number of inconsistencies which though they told heavily against him did not amount to proof. The matter of the clothing being found west of Santa Monica was possibly explicable by the theory that they could have been caught in a riptide and taken far offshore to a west-going current.

"You've got to remember that all a defendant has to do is show reasonable doubt and he must be judged innocent," said Minardi. "And I suppose that a riptide in some twenty miles of coastline could be said to be a reasonable doubt."

Father Bredder shook his big head. "Santa Monica is a heavily used beach," he said. "So is Malibu beyond. Even if the clothes were caught in a riptide and carried away from the shore, the chances are huge that some swimmer or boater or fisherman would have come on them. But Johnson had those clothes all the time. He or Littleton found them right after Kestion left them on the beach—within twenty-four hours. The clothes were Kestion's alibi to show that he was at Santa Monica when Susan was killed. The alibi could be established by a time sequence. By removing the alibi, Littleton was able to direct suspicion against Kestion. Johnson's mistake was to restore the alibi when both Kestion and Littleton were dead. He thought it would be tidier to throw all the blame on Littleton and tidy things up by finding Kestion's clothes. So he suddenly announced that he had found them—at a place where they could not have been found except by a freak."

Minardi made no comment on this immediately. He was thinking of Kestion and Susan—the poet with the dead soul and the girl with the dead heart. They were hardly deadly enemies. "Even destroying his alibi, Littleton couldn't have made much of a case against Kestion," he said.

"He knew that," said the priest. "But if he killed him and made it look like suicide or death by misadventure, then he didn't have to prove a case. It was easily done. He contacted Kestion after Susan's death. He knew Kestion was a drug user. Kestion had said so in his lecture. He just had to hint at his sympathy with the drug cult and mention that he knew of a safe source of supply—namely himself—and he had Kestion."

"But Kestion thought the chief was going to frame him and asked you to help him," said Minardi.

"That came later," said Father Bredder. "When Kestion realized that his clothes were never going to be found and his alibi was gone."

"And he would still trustingly take drugs from Littleton?" said Minardi. Father Bredder made no reply and Minardi, staring at him, lowered his head.

"I know," he said. "They'll take them from anybody—even people who have sold them junk. There comes a time when they lose the ability to reason and they believe only what they want to believe—horoscopes, lucky charms, dogs-are-superior-to-people, and paradise-is-to-be-found-in-a-pill. You know, Father, I always thought Anti-Christ would be a person. Turns out he's a complex of chemicals and lives in a little gelatine capsule."

Father Bredder brought forward other details pointing to the lieutenant's guilt. There was the fact that the lieutenant, in charge of the immediate investigation of the murder of

153

Susan Hatfield, had dug up the rose garden searching for a weapon but had delayed twenty-four hours in draining or dredging the goldfish pond. There was the curious circumstance that when the priest and the lieutenant arrived at the Green Bay Tree Café to rescue Barbara, the café was empty —on the word of Lieutenant Johnson—though, as Father Bredder pointed out, a side door of the kitchen was open and it was surely risky for Littleton to have left Barbara in the refrigerator without having someone on guard to see that she was not released by a chance visitor. Señor Chili, the priest theorized, had been on guard and hiding in the cellar and when Father Bredder took Barbara out of the kitchen, the lieutenant had allowed Señor Chili to leave.

Lastly there was the death of Chief Littleton. It evolved that Lieutenant Johnson was an expert pistol shot and a member of a private pistol club. Littleton had been shot twice by Johnson—one shot very near the heart and the other below the right eye. The latter was immediately fatal, but the first would have been fatal in a matter of minutes. So Johnson had shot to kill though that was not necessary and, an expert with a pistol, he could have shot merely to disable.

But all this, though it provided suspicion, did not provide the kind of proof needed in court. And then Señor Chili was arrested and, on a promise of leniency, testified fully against the lieutenant. What he had to say added little to what Father Bredder had already deduced—that the lieutenant was a co-conspirator with Littleton in the sale of the drugs, that he saw to it that the Green Bay Tree Café was not investigated, but Johnson was opposed to murder and the most he would agree to do was cover up for Littleton.

"You know something," said Señor Chili, who turned out

to be quite a philosopher, perhaps as the result of many years in prison, "people do something wrong and then they get kind of fascinated by it and they can't hardly resist doing it again. I mean it seems such a handy solution when a problem comes up. Like you take murder. Chief Littleton slugged that man you say was the girl's father right in the cellar of that café. He'd thought it all out, and I was in on it. We put those old clothes on him and put him in the refrigerator and he was cold, if he wasn't dead, when I took him out and put him up on the embankment in the dark in time for a freight to run over him. About fifty cars. Of course after the first three sets of wheels, it don't matter how many more there are.

"It worked dandy. No identification. Just a bum. So when the daughter wondered about her father being missing just after he arrived and contacted her, then the chief turned to the same solution and figured on another murder. Then, of course, there had to be another murder—that poet feller— and so on. You get stuck in a kind of groove and solve every problem in the same way. In a way it's like me and that chili. I got in a habit of cooking with chili and here I am, headed right back to the stir. And the chief got in a habit of murder —and he's murdered himself now."

But no charge of murder could be brought against Johnson, who himself confessed to the narcotics charge. A more serious charge of conspiracy to conceal the identity of a murderer was not pressed. "As a cop he'll have a hard enough time in jail anyway," said Minardi. "It's a pity. He was a good man. I was getting to like him."

Two months later, in August, Father Bredder received several dozen rhizomes of iris from Mrs. Shepherd and just before school started again he, with Lietuenant Minardi and

Barbara, went to the San Diego Zoo for a day—an annual outing to which they all three looked forward. And while they were looking at the bears, Barbara suddenly said, "Mary Beag, that's who."

"That's who what?" asked her father.

"That's who was in Susan Hatfield's bed. I was looking at the bears and thinking of Little Red Ridinghood and I remembered the toothpaste cap."

"What toothpaste cap?" asked Minardi patiently.

"It was stuck in the hand basin when I got up the following morning," said Barbara. "And I remember when I was talking to Mary Beag and she was asking me about being a policeman's daughter, she said she had trouble because she was careless and couldn't remember to do things that weren't important—like putting the cap back on a tube of toothpaste."

The priest and the detective exchanged glances. "You know, Father," said Minardi, "one of the great advantages of priestly celibacy is that you never have to follow the workings of the feminine mind."

But Father Bredder said quite seriously, "It makes perfect sense to me," and Barbara squeezed his big hand and said, "I knew it would. You always understand."